A Whiter Shade of Pale /
Becoming Emma

A Whiter Shade of Pale

Becoming Emma

TWO NOVELLAS

by
Caterina Edwards

NeWest Press, Edmonton

First Edition

Canadian Cataloguing in Publication Data

Edwards, Caterina, 1948-
  A whiter shade of pale

  ISBN 0-920897-21-5

  I. Title. II. Title: Becoming Emma.
PS8559.D83W5 1992   C813'.54   C92-091454-3
PR9199.3.E38W5 1992

CREDITS
COVER DESIGN: Burgess/Michalchuk Design
INTERIOR DESIGN: Bob Young/BOOKENDS DESIGNWORKS
EDITOR FOR THE PRESS: Mort Ross
FINANCIAL ASSISTANCE: NeWest Press gratefully acknowledges the financial assistance of Alberta Culture and Multiculturalism, The Alberta Foundation for the Arts, The Canada Council, and The NeWest Institute for Western Canadian Studies.

Printed and bound in Canada by Best Gagné Book Manufacturers.

NeWest Publishers Limited
#310, 10359 - 82 Avenue
Edmonton, Alberta
T6E 1Z9

This is a book of fiction and all characters are fictional.

For my mother and father

Parts of these novellas were written with the
financial assistance of the Canada Council and
the Alberta Foundation for the Literary Arts.
I must also thank Mort Ross,
a prince among editors.

A Whiter Shade of Pale

With a special thank you to Dr. Helena Fracchia,
who guided me through the mysteries of
Etruscan art.

For Brian and Nancy

But to the tombs, to the tombs!   D.H. Lawrence

One of the most prevalent misconceptions about the Etruscans is that their language is indecipherable. In fact Etruscan, written in a simple variant of the Greek alphabet introduced via Cumae, can easily be read by anyone even slightly familiar with the Greek alphabet. It is understanding Etruscan that presents problems, since it is of unknown origin and cannot with certainty be related to any groups of known languages.

Mario Torelli

First of all, you should know, George was not a Willie Nelson fan, not since Willie got into that middle-of-the-road crap. When George wanted country, he went for Hoyt Axton, Commander Cody, Asleep at the Wheel, western swing. So his happening to hear the song, his happening to really listen was just chance.

It was his monthly night out. At supper, Cynthia had made a fuss. "This is not the night to go out and leave me."

"It never is, not as far as you're concerned. But you go out. Just last night," he said.

"Oh sure, to the babysitting co-op. Big deal."

"We agreed," he said. "You agreed."

"Not tonight. Why can't you understand?" Her voice was steady, but she was crying.

"If I hadn't been the one to set it up. . . ." He meant to touch her, to show that he did understand. She was standing right beside him, clearing the table. He leaned towards her. She turned suddenly. The edge of the ceramic bowl in her hand hit the side of his face. It was nothing: thirty seconds of pain. "No need to get nasty," he said, and she managed a smile.

Briefly, very briefly, George considered staying home. But it was his evening; he was entitled. And he had been the one to convince his two colleagues, Bob and John, to drive out to the Transit Hotel to catch an appearance by his latest favourite, the then little known k.d. lang. How could he back out? It was going to be good: knock back a few, exchange a few laughs, relax.

Or so he hoped. Once there, once seated around a small table with Bob and John, seeing their less than delighted faces, seeing their dutiful sips, he knew he'd made a mistake. George downed two glasses of beer, one right after the other.

"Great idea," Bob said.

"Trust George," John added.

"Wait till you hear her. She's got a voice," George said.

"Always on the cutting edge, eh?" John said.

"I hope so." George grabbed another glass. I used to be, he thought, once upon a time, in the know. And looking around the worn tavern, he wished he had come alone. He could have sat and drank and listened in peace. With Bob and John and their endless comments, he couldn't concentrate on k.d.: singing, twisting, leaping.

"Quite a place," one would yell. "Talk about energy," the other would yell.

> Work your fingers to the bone
> What do you get?
> Boney fingers, boney fingers.

George sang along under his breath. "BONNNEEYYY fingers." Several of the groups at the tables around them were singing aloud, momentarily united. "Boney fingers –"

His monthly night out. On the way to the can, he tried to sidestep two shouting men only to be caught up in their fight. The bigger of the men clipped the jaw of the other. He, in turn, reacted with flailing fists, one of which struck George on the shoulder. "Hey," George said. The bigger one shoved; the other fell back, and George was slammed against the wall.

Instinctively, George shoved back. Space, he needed space, and air; he needed to be rid of the sandbag flesh, the stink of old sweat and beer, the muttered obscenities. He shoved back all the limits, the restraints. Until hands were hauling him up and off. The bouncer had him by the arm. "All of you – out," the man said.

"Wait. It wasn't – " George began. He caught a glimpse of John and Bob, still sitting comfortable and smug at their table. Such camaraderie, George thought. And he let himself be led out.

His monthly night out. The high life. He parked the car outside his garage and sat, reluctant to turn off the engine. A minute or two and I'll go in, he thought. He was tired, distracted, his face ached. Yet it was then that the first notes of the song insinuated their way through his fatigue.

> We skipped the light fandango
> Turned cartwheels, 'cross the floor ©

Even over the radio, Nelson's voice breathed irony, regret, a deep weariness. Yet, at first, it was not the modest voice, but the song itself, George's cup of Proustian tea, that unleased the sense of elsewhere and other.

A soft summer night. A Roman night. A hard-edged metal and plastic disco. On the stage a three hundred pound crooner with a Supremes-type backup and all around, tricky and dazzling, dancers and lights, fandangoed indeed. Jackie, intoxicated by their cleverness in having found Rome's most fashionable night spot, the Piper Club, pronounced peeper as she reminds George at least three times, is clumsily trying to copy the steps, the movements of the surrounding exotica. Start, pause, go, giggle, pause, start. "Can't wait to tell them," she begins at the first break. "I can imagine their evening: 'Let's go raise hell in the piazza' – as if any of them knew what raising – " George cuts her off, pulling her to him, hand around her waist. The flashing lights are replaced by a pink haze. And then, the song. Not the first time he has heard it but the first time he's taken it in, drinking until he was replete with the melody. A Roman night, a dated pop tune, and beneath the surface recall, catacombs of meaning and memory.

"What now?" Cynthia asked when she saw him.

"I guess I am a bit early."

Cynthia was sitting in an armchair at the opposite end of the living room. "Early? Your face. That's what I mean." She was in her nightgown, her thick dark hair down. a glass of milk in hand, but she looked anything but relaxed.

"You whacked me with that dish at supper."

"Oh my God. I didn't think. . . ."

"Then, at the Transit. . . ." George explained what had happened.

"You see. You see. Why don't you ever listen to me? We'll have to concoct some story for the children."

"A story?"

"We can hardly say 'your father was in a barroom brawl.'"

"I was not in a brawl. A guy fell on me."

"I spend most of my days trying to stop Sean from trying to bash the other two with his truck or Jane from biting or. . . . And what really amazes me is that you're the one who talks about non-violence, who said no spanking, who talked of example. You. Example. What kind of example?"

"It was an accident. Anyway, I don't think I was hit on the face in the bar. So can the hysteria. Accept your responsibility." George tried a smile, winced, and pressed his bruised right cheek.

"You look terrible."

"I need a drink."

"I suggest aspirins and milk."

Her face was finally softening. George crossed the room to her chair.

"I just can't believe that I. . . ."

His hands were only inches away from her slim, tanned shoulders. "How about making it up to me?"

> "The statues are in the museum"
> " – No, they pursue you, why can't you see it?
> I mean with their broken limbs.
> With their shape from another time, a shape you don't
>   recognize
> yet know."
>
> Seferis, "Sensual Elpenor," *Thrush II*

No, George thinks, I recognize but I don't know: the shape, the letters and yes, above all, the statues.

* * *

The next afternoon, George did try to work. He was supposed to finish a rough draft of a bill banning extra billing by doctors for a meeting with the Deputy Minister in three days' time. But his mind refused to manufacture the necessary legalese. Neither the statute books nor the computer printouts of similar laws in other provinces helped. He could read the words, repeat them, rearrange them but they remained sounds and signs, a foreign language. He was tired, each of the children had been up in the night, and his face hurt.

"Skip the light," "Quite a place," "All of you – out": unbidden and insistent, these phrases played over and over, like a chorus of a popular song. Then, came another melody: "Civitavecchia, Veii, Tarquinia. Atria, Cupra, and Volterra."

A beach. Lying under a sun umbrella with Jackie, surrounded by Italian families. No glimpse of the sea. Sweet warm Asti. He holds the bottle high so it pours half drink, half shower, doubly refreshing. Another bottle waiting in the sand, his and Jackie's fingers beginning to intertwine. Mamas calling their children away.

His first and probably his only custom made silk shirt. A pale, pale blue. Julian cajoled him into entering the dark, dignified shop, into submitting to being measured, to testing the touch of different silks with his dig-roughened hands. "Why not?" Julian says again, "you're not in Edmonton now. No one knows you. Pretend you're Gatsby."

The work of the dig. First picks, moving the dirt with wheelbarrows. Then, past 2,000 years of dirt, more precisely, smaller picks, then dental instruments and sieves. Each era a distinct layer, each layer a different pile of dirt. Slowly, carefully, feeling the different textures of the soil with the fingers. Learning to recognize the man-made by touch. For two summers after Rome. Layer beneath layer down to virgin soil.

His northern skin red, blisters on his back. The sun something to be shielded from. The ever-present dust, grit on his sensitive skin, cracks between his toes. "And old, old, old fungus," he had told Jackie, "from some Etruscan athlete."

A trip to Tarquinia. A shared lunch amid some Roman ruins. Jackie, Sophie, and Julian. Bread and ham, peaches and wine. Bleached stones and oleanders. A fallen altar their table, column stumps their chairs. Sophie stringing blossoms in her long, dark braid. Jackie breaking the bread. "Take this and eat."

> "Really, those statues are not
> the fragments. You yourself are the relic;
> They haunt you with a strange virginity
> at home, at the office, at the receptions for the
>   celebrated,
> in the unconfessed terror of sleep:"
> Seferis, *Thrush II*

The first summer on the dig, George is one of sixteen students digging under the direction of three professional archaeologists seven hours a day, six days a week for eight weeks. During that summer, the group unearths countless loom weights, part of a wall, one gold earring, and a child's sarcophagus.

* * *

A random scattering of red dots on a white page. Blood, his blood. He'd been so given over, he hadn't noticed his nose beginning to bleed.

George had his head up, was pinching his nose, swabbing with Kleenex and smiling at himself and his ruminations when Bob knocked at his door.

"How's it going?"

"As you can see."

"Jesus, that sleaze really hit you."

"No. . . . I'm not sure. I took a little knock a bit earlier. Hey, you and John were a big help. If you'd explained to the bouncer. And you didn't even come out and see how I was. I could have been hurt."

Bob dropped into a chair in front of the desk. "It happened so fast. We were both shocked. . . . But we thought it best to hang back. I mean, it could have . . . what if it kept on? What if there was a rumble? How would it have looked?"

"Right. A rumble." George shrugged a "forget it." The blood was stopping.

"You were smiling when I came in."

"Ummm. Can I do anything else for you? Or are you only here to survey the damage."

"I did want to ask you something. I was going to mention it last night but then. . . ." Bob fiddled with a cigarette pack and some matches. "Rumour has it that Blanfield-Jones has decided to take the Ottawa job."

"So I've heard."

"And rumour has it that you have the inside track."

So, that was it. "Really."

Bob dropped his casual, sprawled posture. "Would you accept?"

"Accept. I haven't even applied. . . . Why do you think I have the inside track?"

"You're the golden boy. I mean, the Deputy Minister often asks for you specifically and, well, you've been here a long time."

"Don't remind me. I never imagined. . . . But then I never imagined myself a lawyer either."

"And here you are." Bob was not going to let himself be deflected into a discussion of what George had imagined. Bob had an agenda and was following it. "With seniority."

"Surely not. There are others. . . ." George didn't like to admit that most of the other legislative draftsmen were younger than he.

"None that they'll look at seriously. I'm sure I don't have to spell it out for you. Come on George, drop the coyness. Are you interested or not?"

"I suppose." George's swollen nose was filling. "Why not?" As he grabbed for the Kleenex box, the blood sank through his mustache to his lips.

* * *

" 'they speak of things you wish didn't exist
or would exist years after your death,
And that's difficult because . . .'"

                    " – The statues are in the museum
Good night."

"because the statues are no longer
fragments. We are. The statues bend lightly. . . . Good
    night."

At this point they separated. . . .
                    Seferis, *Thrush II*

Another known, unknowable alphabet, he thinks, another.

* * *

It was on the High Level bridge, on his walk home that George realized he was suffering from more than a nosebleed. His legs were heavy. He almost had to order them to move. The narrow path became a tight rope; he was balanced between the lights of creeping cars and the blackness of the valley. Halfway across, as the ice-dusted wind blew stronger, the long steel lines began to wave, to shift. He clung to a girder, clung, everything spinning, clung, so the winds of panic wouldn't carry him off, down then up, down to the frozen river, flinging him up, up till a final crash against the hard lights of the city.

A new gush of blood, warm and wet on his face. The spin slowing down, the path righting itself. He would concentrate on his feet, only watch his feet. One in front of the other. The bridge stretched endlessly. Would he ever get off? The creak of cars, the smell of fumes, long, long bridge. A careful balance.

Home. One foot in front of the other. Balance. But when he finally unlocked the door, finally stepped into the warmth and the light, there was no rush of children, no flurry of words and hugs, no signs of supper.

Cynthia was sitting in the living room, in the armchair, a Bandaid-covered Sean on her lap. Jane and Sarah were at her feet, one slowly ripping a magazine, the other chewing on her favourite stuffed bunny. George could barely pick his way through the scattered books, toys, and crayons.

"Thank God you're home. I have had the most awful day."

"Mine," George, clearing a spot so he could sit on the

sofa, brushed off a pile of wooden puzzle pieces, "wasn't too great either."

"I was rushing around all morning, trying to get errands done, took the stroller to Friendly Bears to be fixed, went to the bakery, cleaners, Safeway. The kids got bored in the car. Jane started screeching. Sean hit her with his truck. She got cut, yes, there, on the cheek. Then they all screeched."

George began massaging his neck. "Oh no." His tone was offhand, almost uninterested.

Cynthia shot him one of her glances but continued. "Sean kept pulling off his jacket and hat. I had visions of pneumonia, after last year. So I'd stop and climb in the back. It was dreadful, just dreadful. When I got home, Michael refused to leave the car. Pulled his rigid routine. So I left him inside while I carted the other two and all the stuff in. When I got back, he was turning blue, screaming and dear Mr. Slough was standing by the car. He lit into me about the dangers of leaving a child."

"Poor you." George had let his head roll back so that it rested on the sofa back. He spoke with his eyes closed.

"It went on and on. Oh, I forgot, Jane pulled down a pile of cans in Safeway. At lunch – here comes the exciting part – Sarah decided to push her vitamin pill up her nose and she did. Just like that. Then Michael, before I could stop him. I was worried, but then they started to melt. Orange goop dripping from two noses. At least it wasn't beads like last week. Then they refused to nap. Just whined and fought all afternoon. I get so bored I can't think. About an hour ago Michael fell down the stairs. I thought his nose was broken until he stopped yelling."

Michael and Jane had crawled over to their father. "Da-da, Daddy."

"My Daddy. Mine. He likes me."

"Sure do. Both of you. All of you."

"So what happened? What ruined your day? You're obviously too overwhelmed to pay any attention to my problems."

"I got a nosebleed."

"A nosebleed?" Cynthia seemed genuinely incredulous. "That's all? Anyway if you didn't go and get beaten. . . ." She glanced down at Sarah.

"I didn't get . . . whatever. I won."

"Men, you're all crazy."

That night his nose again began to bleed. "Cyn," he gasped. She kept her head on her pillow.

"Cyn," George was grabbing for the tissues, turning on the side light.

"Whaat?" When she flipped over, opened one eye and saw his pillow, then she took notice. She brought wet flannels to lay on his nose, a towel for the flow. "Sit up more. Calm down. Try deep breathing. That'll help."

It didn't.

"I guess I better go into emergency."

"Stay calm. You're too tense."

George was pulling on his clothes with one hand. "Can you call the cab?"

Cynthia was silent for a long moment. "I spent all the cash today. Can't you drive? It's so close."

* * *

On the dig, he grows skilled at sensing what was simply stone and what was relic. The nerves in the ends of his fingers recognize the traces of human intention and will. By touch, he knows. By touch.

* * *

He drove slowly, looking both ways at each empty intersection, focusing completely on parking the car neatly between a truck and an Oldsmobile in the lot. He was pleased he could make his body walk steadily into emergency and fill out the forms. He wasn't made to wait. He probably looked too messy. He'd hardly sat down, between a muttering drunk and a woman joggling a whining baby, when he was whisked off to a room.

The round-faced intern asked no questions. He walked over to George, pulled away the towel and thrust his light and then his fingers up George's nose. George had to breathe in and out slowly, concentrating on expanding his abdomen, so as not to give in to his urge to pummel that big, childlike head.

"Can't see much."

"It starts and stops."

"Nurse, we'll need more gauze."

"Why would it. I mean, why would I bleed so much?"

"A little blood looks like a lot."

"But a tap by a plate yesterday? My wife and I both turned at the wrong moment. Why would I bleed today?"

"We'll take care of it in a jiffy."

"Last night it happened."

The intern was arranging the instruments. "I wondered. This seems the week for battered . . . for family conflicts. Now, hold still. Don't be embarrassed. These things happen. A few drinks too many."

George would have laughed if the metal prongs hadn't been up his nose. "Aahh."

The intern stepped back, cocked his big head to one side, surveying. "You weren't drinking, but you had a bad day."

"No. I did drink, but later."

"You were drinking. And your wife with you."

"No. No."

"She wasn't drinking and that added to the tension."

"I was at. . . ." George could no longer speak. Yards and yards of gauze were being shoved up his nose and into his sinus. His head was literally being stuffed.

"You should consider AA. Drinking creates problems; it doesn't solve them. There. That'll hold you." The intern paused at the door. "The nurse has some leaflets you can read. Be careful. Redheads have a predisposition to bleeding. Vascular insufficiency."

* * *

The second summer at the dig, in the north-east corner of a villa, underneath the broken roof tiles, underneath the collapsed walls, they discover dozens upon dozens of miniature votive statues. Offerings to the household gods, offerings to ensure protection, to avert calamity from the house, the family. Comforting, the idea of household gods, the supposition that a terracotta statue could buy security.

The next morning, Cynthia suggested he stay home. "You must be tired. Besides you need to relax."

"How much rest could I get here?" His gesture took in the cluttered table, the filled sink, the jam-smeared children. "Around here, every time I lie down, someone jumps on me."

"You admit it. Your work is an escape. It's harder to be home. Harder for me."

"I am very busy. Session starts in two weeks."

"I bet."

So, though he was already running late, he told her about Bob and the prospective job.

"Work your fingers to the bone
What do you get?
Boney fingers."

"Daddy," Michael's face was scrunched up partly in thought, partly in protest against the dishrag. (He was last in line. Cynthia was wiping fingers and faces.) "You don't get bony fingers because they're already bony. See, feel mine."

"Cynthia you missed a spot here. You know Michael, you're right. Bony fingers."

Michael kept his spread fingers before his father's face. "Bones."

Cynthia grabbed him by the shoulders and guided him out the door. "All of you. Time for Hercules." She was usually wordless and as close to motionless as possible in the morning. All the forcefulness and activity, she was now refilling their coffee cups, signalled her disquiet. "Do you really want this job?"

"Want?"

"You're so busy as it is. But if you really wanted, if I could understand. . . ."

"The salary. . . . It's the way it works, Cyn." What he had at first taken to be her disquiet, he now realized was a deeper, broader unease. He pushed away his cup. He could not sit and discuss the job or the nosebleed or, worse, their lives. He could not. "Look, I'm already about half an hour late."

"You do have an excuse."

"I said I had a lot to do."

* * *

No, I recognize but I don't know: the shape, the letters, the statues.

* * *

He worked well until mid-afternoon. The phrases came quickly as if legal jargon was the only language he knew. Then, at mid-afternoon, he lay down his pen, intending to break for coffee, stretched and abruptly fell into a waiting dream.

He was standing before an enormous mound of dirt, holding a shovel. Cynthia was by his side, bent over, shovel in the dirt. "Bedrock."

"We'll never manage." Side by side, lifting the dirt.

"Ashes to ashes indeed." Julian was with them, not working, rolling up the sleeves of his blindingly white shirt. "Each era, just two feet of dust."

"Watch the bones."

Jackie stood at the top of the mound, a bottle in each hand. "I'll take care of it in a jiffy." Unscrewing each cap and pouring. "I'll take care of it all." The scent of white wine and dust, Jackie laughing, her lips pulled back in a near grimace. Julian rolling up his white sleeves. The scent of wine and dust. Cynthia wiping the sweat from her neck and shoulders.

George awoke suffused with a sense of well-being. He fumbled in his vest pocket, pulled out his gold watch and held it up at an angle, all without lifting his head. Twenty to three. Five minutes since he had last checked and yet he had slept, he had dreamt. "Each era. . . ."

A curb in the village above the dig. Night after night. Sitting between Jackie and Julian, passing a bottle of *Est! Est! Est!* Past midnight, the nightly parade of youths in the *passeggiata* had dissipated. Their voices, their laughter echoes against the empty piazza, the shuttered houses and shops. Their conversation begun several hours and several bottles before in the trattoria is so earnest, so sincere. Life, death, love. Ideals – "To the stars" – under the stars and the velvety night.

The first friendships of adulthood – the elation springing not from the shared bottle but from shared thought, from the first common flexings of the mind.

But why was he remembering now? He stared out the window, doodled and paced. He couldn't stop. He was shaking the fragments of recall free from the dirt of everyday memories. He was assembling them, like artifacts, arranging, mounting, labelling for mental exhibition so that encased, they glowed, signs of past knowledge, past happiness.

He had been eighteen years old. It was his first time away from family and home, his first place where he knew no one and was known by no one. In that first isolation, in that first lack of connection to the parade of sights, tastes, and sensations, there was an intoxicating freedom. He could invent himself for his new companions, present himself as he wished to be, and now was, a man.

George had always been aware of the dangers of constantly looking back, hating his father's phrases "in my day" and "the good old days." Was it inevitable that he lose that wariness with age? Inevitable that he be seduced by nostalgia and its deceitful, golden light?

Sun, dry heat, dust. Out of the sun, in the cool, labyrinthine halls of the museum, in the dark tombs of Cerveteri, he loses himself. Before the funerary statues, before the peeling frescoes, the personal falls away. He can decipher no message from the art of these mysterious, long dead people. Yet he is stunned, captivated.

Civitavecchia, Veii, Tarquinia, Cupra, it was becoming a chant. And the true inevitability was the sudden wetness at his nose.

John drove him to the hospital but didn't offer to come in with him. There was a longer wait this time; the blood was more a trickle than a gush. George flipped through *Vogue* and *Town and Country*, looking for nudes, then read the restaurant reviews for both Edmonton and Calgary in six back issues of *Western Living*.

When the nurse finally called him, she mispronounced his name, so he didn't respond until the third call. All the other prospective patients lifted their heads or turned and stared at him and the tissue at his nose. And the doctor, a tiny woman with light, frizzy hair, when he answered her "What can I do for you today?" repeated "a nosebleed" a bit incredulously. Still, her hands were gentle as she pulled the length of bloodied gauze from his sinus caverns. "Extraction and repacking," she told the nurse. "There should be no recurrence."

* * *

"We believe that lightning is caused by clouds colliding, whereas they believe that clouds collide in order to create lightning . . . they are led to believe not that events have a meaning because they have happened, but that they happen in order to express a meaning."

Seneca, *Naturales Quaestiones II*

"It must be psychological," Cynthia pronounced three days and two trips to the hospital later. "If you would calm down."

"Come on. Don't give me that shit." George cupped his hands around his very sore, much prodded nose, dabbing lightly at the drips.

When he and Cynthia had first fallen in love, she, like many of their friends, had an analyst. At first he thought it was not much more than an affectation. They all sat around on the blue carpet outside the s.u. theatre, eating their brown-bag lunches, dissecting each other's motives, each other's essential selves. Words like "hostile," "repression," and "male ego" buzzed in and about the sandwiches and chocolate cake. My analyst thinks, my analyst says, my analyst, a prop in the adolescent search for significance. But, as they became George and Cynthia, he began to judge her analyst, that unknowable other male, as a more sinister force. Through the elation and the discoveries, through the long walks and the long nights, through their tentative mapping of what they as a couple would be, part of Cynthia was unconnected.

"I can't explain," she would say, or "I can't talk about it." Yet it seemed to George that her private journey cast its shadow over both of them, twisting her moods and his responses.

Afterward – they were living together by then – she did try to explain. And he could see that a certain edginess, a certain frantic tone was gone. Still, George couldn't help wondering whether they wouldn't have faded anyway, whether the journey hadn't been artificially set.

"I'm not seeing any analyst."

"O.K. . . . Ask them to give you some tranquillizers then. Anti-anxiety pills."

"Anyone would be tense if they kept bleeding. You always have to categorize everything as psychological. Remember that time you kept passing out on the floor and you kept insisting it was psychological and it turned out you were anemic."

Cynthia smiled. She began collecting his discarded wads of Kleenex. "I've been reading this article."

"In the *New Yorker*?"

"What else do I have the time or concentration for these days?"

"*Vogue. Glamour.* In which case I'd discount what you are about to say. Articles from women's magazines are inapplicable."

"Sexist. Anyway, it says that Freud believed, at first, that you could treat mental disturbances by treating the nose. You could operate on say the sinuses and relieve hysteria."

"I always said he was a charlatan."

"He also believed in the healing powers of cocaine, applied to the nose, of course."

"We should be so lucky."

"Maybe you can connect parts of the nose to specific bits of the brain, sort of like reflexology." She called this out from the kitchen where she'd gone to deposit the tissues.

"I don't see why you're so cheerful about all this. It's getting serious."

She was back with a wet cloth. "I know, George. It's just, you have to see. It's also getting ridiculous." She lay the cold cloth across his forehead, and George had to resist the impulse to toss it across the room.

"Back to emergency."

"I don't know."

They gazed at each other across the expanse of living room, suddenly suspended, unsure. And finally, one of the children did yell out. And, as Cynthia got up, the phone did ring.

"The difference between the Romans and the Etruscans is this: We believe that lightning is caused by clouds colliding, whereas they believe that clouds collide in order to create lightning . . ."

By touch, he knows, by touch.

A nose is a nose is a nose is a nose.

Isn't it?

No one, in the days of the blue carpet and the endless analysis, ever analysed Julian. He was Troilus; he was Jake Barnes; he was a dozen other romantic heroes – or so they all thought. Julian was classically handsome and obviously troubled for he wore his superiority, his taste, his sensitivity, rather than his heart, on his sleeve. And even professors noted for their vulgar turns of phrase became fanciful before him. "Byron, the spitting image."

Julian, George, and James, a drama student and Julian's best friend from high school, shared a suburban three bedroom house for several of their university years.

They all "did" drugs. Those were the times. Anything going by they tried. "Good for a buzz." "Far out stuff." Grass, acid, M.D.A, hashish oil, magic mushrooms, peyote buttons, opium, and coke.

But none of it had much effect on Julian. While the other two were flying, he would be merely at the edge of nearly feeling something, nearly seeing. So he drank: tumbler after tumbler, bottle after bottle of Greek brandy. And, as the booze disappeared, he would become more controlled and more acerbic, insisting on replacing a Procol Harum record with Mozart, ridiculing a hairdo or a philosophy, a guest or his poem. Cool, arrogant Julian. Still you never knew he was drunk until he passed out, his 6 foot 1 inch frame suddenly bisecting the living room or blocking the door to the bathroom. George and James had to work out a routine for moving Julian. He was heavy despite his slimness. "Solid bones," James would say, slipping his hand under the inert knees. "Iron bones," George's hands under the armpits. "now, one, two, three."

After Jackie left Julian, his drinking lost any link with companionship or youthful play. He was serious about brandy and tinkering with all the rest. George was living in Ottawa with Cynthia by then, articling in the Solicitor General's department so his knowledge of Julian during this time was fragmentary, culled from the letters of mutual friends. Bright Julian failing grad school. Fastidious Julian sinking into sloth in a filthy apartment. Discerning Julian was out every night not with his old friends, some of whom he'd known since kindergarten and who, after all, counted on him, but a new fast bunch. "Edmonton's answer to the jet set," suggested Ted, who was retreating himself, but into Buddhism. Julian's new group loudly declared its dedication to art: they bought Warhol's silkscreen of Gretzky (before Warhol died and the price went up); they flew down to Calgary for any opening of "international" art shows at the Glenbow; they helped organize the fund-raising Christmas Holly Ball at the Edmonton Art Gallery ("such ambiance, and the trees! Each decorated to a different theme!"). But their dedication never extended as far as supporting or buying the work of young or not so young local artists. "One of them does these ink drawings of their favourite watering holes. They buy those, but that doesn't really count," commented Anne. She had always had a particular interest in Julian and was mournful in her report that he was dropping hints about what he called his lifestyle (just six months before he would have been embarrassed to use such a word), hints about three-way swings and orgies.

Julian, still the hero, was rescued by the love of a good woman. If a girl had led him into the swamps of love, leaving him without a map and without a boat, it was a woman, older, yes, married, yes, mother of four, who appeared with the canoe and reawakened his sense of direction. Iris was small-boned and gentle-voiced, lace and cameos and lavender cologne, not at all the solid, sensible woman George, well all of them, expected. Still, she divorced her husband, walked out with the two youngest and the silver. She and Julian opened a U-frame-it shop, which prospered and became two and then three shops. They bought a house, started a commercial gallery and were married in as traditional a ceremony as they could manage.

Julian and George remained friends. They saw each other regularly even though they continued to move in different directions. Julian was spiraling inward and back. Iris was his life, Iris and the pale, polite children and the home they constructed around them, a home that radiated harmony and order. They combined centuries and cultures

– Queen Anne, Victorian, Art Deco, Roman sculpture, and Chinese vases. The past was theirs: a playground, a warehouse, a conquered city. It was theirs; they took only the best, the most tasteful, copies, reproductions on the whole, but still – Venetian masks in the bathroom, Renaissance line drawings in the kitchen. Vermeer, Canaletto, Bonnard. The names of artists were on their lips more frequently than the names of friends. And, when George dropped in on them unexpectedly, he always had the sense he had interrupted an Iris and Julian dialogue. They would be arranged on two facing loveseats, the coffee table between them, each with a neat pile of books, each with a drink, cognac in the winter, gin and tonic in the summer.

"We're on the Ottoman empire now."

"I was remembering all the Art Deco in Budapest and we slipped off into discussing. . . ."

They had slipped off indeed. Hand in hand, floating through the past, through their white rooms, hand in hand, a closed circle, their backs to the present. If George mentioned something current, a football game he'd gone to, the federal elections, a mild expression of embarrassment would flicker over Julian's face. He was not uninformed, of course, but wasn't it all too boring to consider?

So they could stand on their ramparts and look over the hollow where the stream flowed among its bushes, across from the city of life, gay with painted houses and temples, to the near at hand city of their dear dead, pleasant with its smooth walks and stone symbols and painted fronts.

D. H. Lawrence

Not for George and Cynthia. They were signers of petitions, takers of classes, on the executive of the community league and the committee to preserve Old Strathcona. Cynthia in particular, for George had to admit much of the impulse outward had to do with Cynthia; she was always rushing to far-flung corners of the city for an environmental agency or a group to aid depressed mothers. Their phone rang constantly. Friends dropped in. There always seemed to be extra children in the yard or the basement. "I believe in community," she would say with no irony.

"You have to stay and fight," she told Iris and Julian when a proposed freeway threatened their neighbourhood. But they didn't. They sold their house and bought another in a more unassailable district. The remaking of the new house (the raising it to the right level of exquisiteness) took all of Julian's spare time. George hadn't seen him in about six months but Julian, happening to phone that evening to see how they were and learning of George's affliction, insisted on coming over immediately, even if it was late, to drive him to the hospital.

It wasn't until they were both in the car that George noticed, over the nose and the towel, that Julian had changed. He looked more than six months older. There were new lines around his eyes and the white hair was more a massive infusion than a touch at the temples.

"It's been awhile."

"Odd, you calling when you did."

Julian looked pleased. "Telepathy. . . . I'm always here when you need me."

"I know."

"No. Seriously. . . ." He held George's glance.

George could think of no reply. "Damn nose."

"When did it start?"

"Days ago."

"Cynthia said something about a barroom brawl. Wildman George coming to the fore."

"I don't know. . . . I was thinking of Rome. . . . I don't know why."

Julian veered around the corner. The front tire caught some ice. The car began to slide. He whipped the steering wheel around. "Rome. You and I and Jackie." He was drunk. George suddenly saw it in the way he was holding his mouth, pausing slightly before each word.

"Careful!"

Julian laughed. He speeded up, hitting the ever icy intersection at an angle. The car turned completely around. Luckily, the winter streets were empty. "Eternal triangle in the eternal city."

"Will you concentrate on your driving?"

"Shut up, George. Talking makes you bleed. Anyway, I'm right. I remember. We both wanted her. And we both jockeyed madly. And. . . ."

"Julian, the turn. . . ."

"Ummm."

"Try to keep in mind that I'm bleeding to death and you're driving me to the hospital."

"We're here. We're here. If I can just find a place to park. Or do you want to be dramatic? I can barrel up to the emergency entrance."

The waiting room was unusually quiet. There was only a woman with whining child and, on the other side of the square of chairs, a potbellied man wearing a denim jacket with "The Rebels" written across the back and a fresh, deep cut from cheek to chin. George moved slowly between them, carefully lowering himself onto the chair. He had discovered in the parking lot that any sudden movement, any haste, caused the horizontal to veer, the vertical to tip.

Julian didn't sit. He stood in front of George glancing alternately at the woman and child and the wounded man. Under the fluorescent lights, he was swaying ever so slightly. "Riff-raff" he mouthed.

"For God's sake, sit."

He dropped into the chair beside George. His eyes fixed on George's face. He seemed to be waiting for some response.

"She was yours. But then I wanted her. And I took her away." He was speaking in a stage whisper. Both the woman and the man were staring at George.

"Julian, not here."

"You loved her. That's why I was punished."

"I did NOT." He had taken the towel away, exposing his nose to the room.

Julian simply shook his head. He stared and stared, waiting, waiting. George could feel his will, a rock interrupting the stream of pain, demanding something, something indefinable from him.

A nose *is* a nose is. . . .

Are you still reading she says.

History, Greek poetry, in translation of course. A travel book, he says.

Yes, I see what; I'm wondering why, she says.

I told you I was trying to understand – my reaction –

You can't find answers in orderly quotations. Phrases from the past.

Why not?

The context is too different. The text with the text, you know.

Look you aren't my teacher here, now, he says.

I'm just trying to warn you. You think it's a simple process – you pick up an author, read the words and voilà. It's not like that. Their view of the world was so different from ours.

I know that, he says.

Wait, the problems of translation and connotation are enough. But then if you consider the differences in basic assumptions, concepts, thought processes. It goes on and on.

I know it's not easy, he says.

When you read, you are projecting *your* meaning, your life, onto those words.

I was hoping for the reverse.

    Touch   by   touch

      "in two straight lines they went to bed"

In spite of the sleeping pill the nurse gave him, George slept so lightly that he was sure that he hadn't slept at all. All night part of him was aware of the faint light at each of the doors of the ward, of the nurse moving through her rounds with only the odd shoe squeak, of the tidy line of grey mounds, of the body rolled and shoved from a stretcher to the bed opposite (unloaded and strapped in like cargo), aware of the snores, a cacophony of grunts, snorts, and whistles, of the incidental obscenities, sleep talk, aware of the bitter smell: disinfectant and dirt, garlic and booze breath, piss, spunk, sour fear creeping out of hidden creases. Even when he dreamt the now familiar return to the dig, the chip, chipping at a cliff of time, he was oppressed by those rows of other men: continents of flesh, oceans of blood, and he could sense his blood, drip, dripping in the packed caverns of his nose.

One tiny weak spot. That was all. Indeed, all.

Sky blue. A touch of gold. Then, a pale, pretty face: plush lips and dark shadowed eyes. A vision, it had to be; this was no nurse gazing at him from the foot of his bed but a damsel in distress with haunted eyes, trailing garments, and wild flowers in her hair. George tried to sit up. The sudden pain in his head pulled him back down. He opened his mouth, cleared his throat. "Who?" His tongue lay inert, unmoving. "Ahh." Hesitantly, he touched his face, pressing inch by inch. The left side was sore. His right felt nothing, even when he increased the pressure, pushed his fingers into the skin and bone. Odd, they must have given him a local on top of the general anaesthetic. He edged himself up on one elbow. The blue and gold girl had wafted over to the bed to his right.

She was speaking to the quite ordinary looking,

bespectacled man in the bed. "You must get well in time." Her voice was appropriately wispy.

"And the pavilion?"

"Lady Cordelia finished the stitching yesterday."

There was a white flower on his blanket. Hers obviously. But had it been dropped by accident or design? He edged a little higher and stretched out his hand. Paper. A crinkly paper flower.

Still, he completed the gesture, lifting the dead flower to his deadened nose, while gazing at the lady. And she gazed back, she did; until, heralded by clinks and tinkles, the knight appeared: chainmail, a white tunic and a red cross, appeared at her side and bowed to her hand. "At your service."

The sweet scene was interrupted by a roar, an elongated, bellowing roar. It was coming from the bed opposite; the occupant was curved into an airborne arc, straining upwards against the leather restraints. A nurse and an orderly were converging on the bed. Fragments of the roar separated into syllables, then words – foul and disconnected. The nurse jerked the curtain closed. The knight, the lady, and the man with glasses were gone, but the rest of the ward was watching the white undulating canvas. Rage was shading into anguish, the roar into a howl. George waited for a sudden silence but the noise did not stop. The nurse and then the orderly emerged from behind the curtain. They both looked a bit flustered, her cap was at an angle, his mouth was grim, but they walked off without a backward glance. The howl faded very slowly. Now and then it changed pitch, or broke into a word. Gradually it ceased to dominate. It became an unpleasant undertone, a hum. George was not even aware of its subsiding. He only realized it had stopped when the older man in the bed to his left said "at last" and "poor bastard."

In two summers' work, George's group manages to excavate one-twentieth of the area of the ancient town. They uncover two villas, a kiln, and a public square. Of the various objects uncovered in this area, votive statues are by far the most numerous.

By the time Cynthia came to pick him up in the late afternoon, George had been examined by a nurse, an intern, a resident, and two specialists. He had not been given a local, and they had no explanation for the numbness. But they all agreed that he could not be released and that another operation was necessary.

"I can't believe it." Cynthia repeated the phrase at each pause in his explanation. "I can't believe it."

"Odder and odder." George had to shape his lips and tongue for each word.

"Bloody hospital." She said, though she was looking at him as if he planned it.

"Doctors. And then I couldn't get any sleep." George described the night and then the roarer. He gestured at the still closed curtain. "Nothing since. The nurse does check now and then, otherwise you'd think he was dead. Talk about odd. Then there was this woman."

"Woman?"

"Here . . . when I woke from the operation."

"In the men's ward?"

"If I could have a private room."

"Well, I thought you were only here for a day. I didn't. . . ."

"La Belle Dame Sans Merci."

"La who?"

"O What can ail thee, wretched wight/Alone and palely loitering?" This was offered by the man on George's left, who had been reading steadily from a thick blue volume all day. "John Keats at his most vague."

"Mmmm, not quite. There is a part about a girl, isn't there?" His tongue had begun to move more easily, but he still could only feel half of it.

The man closed his book. "'Full beautiful, a faery's child, /Her hair was long, her foot was light/And her eyes were wild.'" He had an upper class English accent and a large, almost bald head.

Cynthia's smile was fixed. She stood up and casually positioned herself by the bed so that her back blocked the man from George's sight. "This is a new you. I thought I was the one with the English degree." She spoke in a lowered tone.

"That's me. Full of surprises," George said, not mentioning that he got it from the back of an old Marianne Faithfull album. "Anyway, this girl was still floating."

"A flower child."

"More than that. I – " George shook his head. "More than that." Alone, he thought, alone and palely loitering.

"You always blow things out of proportion."

"Me?" weakly "You – "

"Well, you give meaning to details that have no meaning. All you need to do is ask the man she was visiting who she is and why does she dress like that."

"I keep saying that's not the point."

"That's him, right?"

The man with glasses was standing at the foot of a bed halfway down the ward. He was talking away to a very old man, a tremulous head on a wattled neck. Cythnia set off; her walk was solid, confident, her legs turned out from so many years of ballet.

"Oh, dear," said the professorial type.

"When she gets. . . ."

"Women."

Cynthia returned with the man in hand. "This is Rolf," she said, "a member of the Society for Creative Anachronisms." She smiled, bent over for a kiss. "I'd like to stay and hear all about it but."

And her eyes indicated she was leaving him to his just reward.

Rolf plonked his long, thin body down on George's bed and sprawled out. George had to draw up his legs. Rolf had already begun the explanation: hierarchy, costumes, jousts. "We are demon researchers." The professor pulled his blanket over his head. "We are so accurate." Knights and ladies, feasts, duels, love tokens, "we reproduce" Rolf's leit motif. And when George thought Rolf was done and was about to ask what was wrong, why was he there, he switched to the world of games. "My job. Inventing them. I make money at it too. Lots." Rolf paused, smiling, obviously waiting for George's expression of amazement.

"Could you sit on your own bed? My legs have gone to sleep."

"Sure. I am sorry. I get so excited." Rolf resettled and recommenced. Play, rules, pretend, pretend, war, dungeons and dragons, swords and sorcerers: fantasy, fantasy. An armour of words clanking through the ward.

* * *

In the museum, the first statue to capture his attention is the head of a youth. The head is of pale golden-coloured stone and, with its thick abundant curls, almond-shaped eyes and hat with turned back brim, characteristically Etruscan. But it is the smile, the gentle, closed curve, that catches him.

The vividness of line and the smile. Afterwards he reads many conflicting descriptions of the archaic smile. It is variously described as cruel, predatory, pagan, ambiguous, empty, and a sign of fulfillment, completion, and wholeness. But, for him, it holds no message. He does not, as Rilke did when gazing on an archaic bust, decide that he must change his life. He knows only that he must look upon it and return to look again.

George lay, eyes closed, waiting for the orderly to take him to surgery. The metal rails on the bed were up, new tubing had been shoved into his arm. From the bed opposite came not a roar but a hoarse monologue. The boy, for when the curtains were pulled back he turned out to be only a long-haired boy, insisted over and over that he had to leave, he had to get out, he had things to do. "A coupla drinks. I just had a coupla drinks."

Even more intrusive was the argument between the professor and the girl visiting him, both of whom were speaking in loud whispers.

"Wake up. These aren't the dark ages."

"It is you who is asleep, not me. If we compare awareness. . . ."

George opened one eye. She had spiky, purple and orange hair. She wore four earrings in one ear and a baggy yellow jumpsuit but her face, no he wasn't mistaken – pouty lips, a delicate nose. The expression, that was different. She was scowling not at the professor but at him, George, as if she had measured him and found him wanting, scowling, her pretty face scrunched up. She couldn't be la belle dame. He was getting old; everyone under twenty was starting to look alike. "It's my life," she whined. Even worse, they were all starting to sound alike.

* * *

The Etruscan language can be read; even the sound of Etruscan is known, only the words are incomprehensible.

Think of Pirandello's *One, No One and A Hundred Thousand*. To go mad from the contemplation of self and reality, to be lost forever in the thickets of doubt convinced you have no self and there is no common reality all because of a chance remark about a nose, all because you realize that others see your nose differently than you do.

Think of Gogol's "The Nose." To awake and have no nose, to meet your nose dressed and walking down the street in full government uniform. Think, *the* nose.

Think a nose is a nose.

Cynthia. His first thought, in the short patches of consciousness in the recovery room, the elevator, the ward. Each time the nurse's hands, checking his pulse and blood pressure, punctuated his sleep: Cynthia. He hated those unknown hands, hated the night sounds of the nine other men, hated their bodies and their breath too close to his. Cynthia, her touch would have been right. When, after one waking, he tried to rise from his bed – he had to pass water or burst – the nurse shoved him back. She pulled a miniature urinal out of the side table, passed it to him. How could he piss with her standing right beside him, watching? His mouth would not shape the words. His head was so heavy, the walls were shifting. And then her hands were upon him. Impersonally upon him. His bladder responded. And he shuddered, down to his very centre he shuddered.

Touch
　　he knows
　　　　by touch.

Yet when George for reassurance conjured up the image of Cynthia, the woman he loved, he did not see her in relation to him. He did not remember her in his arms or beneath his touch. He saw her alone, dancing.

Cynthia had given up ballet before the twins were born. "I'm getting too old. I've had too many injuries. This time, I won't be able to get back," she said and began to cry. The crying continued every night for two weeks. "I can't do it any more. I can't." Nothing he said could divert her. And when he pointed out that her career had been hardly stellar; in fact, it was not really a career at all, and with the children, it was awkward, she cried more intensely. Months later, a television program on dancers, a party with her old colleagues, even a picture of toe shoes in a magazine could start her off again. He would walk into the kitchen and her cheeks would be wet. Or he would find her in bed with the covers over her head. Once he came home to find the children on the rampage and Cynthia locked in the bathroom. When he coaxed her out (with promises that she would not have to cook or clean for at least three days) she emerged clutching an old tutu. "How did I ever fit in this?" she said. "I bet even if I lost all the weight I've gained, I couldn't wear it. I'm sure my rib-cage has expanded since the twins. Was I really this small?"

George kept reminding her that it wasn't as if she had to give up dancing completely. And she'd always been a bit too tall and big boned for ballet. (More tears.) She continued to take modern dance classes, but the tears only stopped when she joined a Spanish dance group. The first Spanish performance, George expected an intensification of the usual transformation that would occur at the ballet performances. And, at first, under the spotlights she did seem totally other: her dress all red ruffles and polka dots, her face brightly painted, her hair brilliantined back into a heavy bun, her strong profile emphasized by two large red flowers behind the ear. But when Cynthia stepped out of the line to dance her solo, when she arched her back, tossed her head, her feet stamping out one complex rhythm, her hands clapping out another both in counterpoint to the dolorous flamenco music, she was not transformed but exposed. This was not Cynthia the mother, the daughter or the wife, but the woman underneath, the essential Cynthia. Her face was rapt, intense, her hips suggestive, all her movements both proud and sensual. The essential Cynthia: her rhythms various, one playing off against the other, her footwork intricate, the melody that moved her hypnotic and foreign, so foreign to him.

"Cynthia."

"Sorry, *c'est moi.*" Julian had pulled the visitor's chair right up beside the bed. He was leaning forward so that his face was only a foot away. The curtain was pulled completely around, the sounds from the rest of the ward muted. "Cynthia asked me to tell you. Michael has that vile flu, and your parents still seem to be away. So you're stuck with me instead of her. I was happy to come of course. Cythnia kept insisting, it was nothing, minor surgery, but I insisted back. I can be stubborn too, my sweet, I said. After all, a mistake has been made. I. . . . Juice? But how are you feeling? What about this side?" Julian lifted his hand to George's face. "Nothing yet? Should I call the nurse? Shouldn't sensation have returned? They've unclamped the nerve. I talked to. . . ."

George draped his arm over his eyes, blocking out Julian's eager eyes.

He was awakened by the nurse's aide and the clanking lunch tray. "I don't. . . ." She was pressing the button at the side of the bed and his top half was being tilted up into a sitting position. "Want." His throat felt scraped, his tongue a heavy slab. "Water. I need."

"There's juice right in front of you." In a plastic cup with a foil top. He fumbled; she watched. He put his mouth to the corner of the cup where he'd managed to remove the foil. The liquid was cloyingly sweet.

"Ueei. Water. Please."

"You'll have to wait." She began moving methodically, passing out the trays down the line.

"Finally. Bloody incompetents." The professor muttered to no one in particular.

The youth opposite was sleeping, his head sporting a new bandage. On George's right, Rolf was ignoring his tray, talking. This time to Julian, who was sitting on Rolf's bed, hunched forward, his chin on his hand. Intent. Yes, definitely intent.

* * *

I wanted the past to cast meaning on my life, he says. O.K. so I was naive. But to give our attention to what has been left to us. That is necessary. Don't argue. It's what you do. What you are.

Argue, me? Just be sure you know what is left, she says.

Yes?

Mute stone   debris.

Not mute. Stone shaped by the hand of man speaks, he says.

But can you understand the language of its utterances?
I – I piece it together – bit by bit.

Ah, the fragments are the letters, she says.

Not even. Parts of one letter. The straight line of the A for example.

You're starting to see. She smiles.

At least to look, he says.

    Laid back. The phrase was too casual for Julian, yet his manner had indeed always been laid, or at least, pulled back. Even that summer in Rome, in cafes, parks, and on curbs, he sat with his body angled away from George and Jackie, and when he spoke in his quiet yet assertive voice, he often stared at the end of his cigarette.
    "All these arches, mausoleums, monuments to battles,wars. I'm tired of them all. Weary to my bones, this Roman imposition. It's heavy, it weighs on one. It's all out of proper proportion. The Greeks now: man as the measure. . . ." Julian framed by a side wall of the Pantheon.

"Oh sure, balance and harmony etc. etc. Spare me. It's just as much a show as the Roman's stuff." Jackie reached across to Julian's pack of cigarettes and, without asking, took one. "Where have you hid your lighter? No, let me cancel what I just said. The Romans were honest. They knew it was all about power and will. And they weren't ashamed to show it." She continued with all the usual about the position of women and slaves in Greece and the less usual about human sacrifices.

When she paused to light up, George plunged in. "But we don't really know what any of them were like. Now and then we get a glimmer, a flash but. . . ."

"I'm speaking of aesthetics here." Julian gestured at the wall behind him.

"You can't understand something out of its context, the meaning. . . ."

Jackie's expression was ever more earnest. She was leaning over the table, threatening the glasses with her sweeping gestures.

"I've heard this part of the discussion before. In fact, I'm tired. . . ." George stopped suddenly. He had almost said something he shouldn't.

Julian edged his chair a bit farther back. "Sure you have, George. In Edmonton, right? Your everyday conversation. Content is nothing. It's the form. No, no, not only the content but the context."

"Don't be so condescending," Jackie said, "about George or about Edmonton."

"Yeah," said George.

"Yeah," said Jackie.

"Soorrry," said Julian. "Now can we get back to the Greeks and Romans?"

"What about the Etruscans? They had something neither the Greeks nor the Romans had."

"What?" Jackie and Julian said in unison.

"It's hard to put in words," said George.

"Hard because it doesn't exist. No, don't bristle, George. I mean it no longer exists. (If it ever did.) It is, as Jackie has been insisting, hard enough to understand the works of art the Greeks and Romans produced and we have a good idea of the context."

"But you were arguing only the form matters."

"I was. I still am. I'm just pointing out that much of the Etruscan world, their monuments, their language has been lost, looted."

"But I'm talking of what has been left: the tombs, the funerary urns, the sarcophagi."

"Exactly, which brings us back to form. And Etruscan form is dull," insisted Julian.

"Never," countered George, "it's vital."

"Commonplace," said Julian.

"Natural," said George.

"In effect, mediocre," said Julian.

"No. You have to look. It doesn't grab you. You have to give in to the experience. You said you were tired of all the imposition."

"Ahh, but I'm not so exhausted that I'm drawn to the middlebrow."

"Middlebrow!"

"Provincial."

It was then that Jackie thrust her arm out and flung her glass of warm milk into Julian's face. "Bloody superior. . . ."

Julian allowed himself no expression of surprise or complaint. He wiped his face with the few paper napkins scattered on the table. "I thought you were for the Romans." He spoke mildly now. "Or is it George's honour?" That second of blindness had opened his eyes; her sensitivity for George changed how he saw her. And how his eyes looked when he looked at her. A few days later, in the Borghese Gardens, George had come back from taking a drink in a nearby fountain to find Jackie asleep on the grass and Julian bent over her, watching.

In retrospect, the debates of youth are embarrassing. With the years, theories give way to details. No longer "what's to be done?" but "what do we do?" How do we survive? Renovations instead of transformations. The men debating indoor tennis or raquetball? More weights? More running? The women arguing the dangers of fat suction, aerobics, tai chi? And for the children – French immersion? Suzuki or Orff? Ballet, jazz, Spanish, folk, or gymnastics? Drama or mime? Clay, collage, drawing or general crafts? The community league is offering a class in creative cooking for seven to ten year olds. The nature centre has eight Saturdays of pioneer experience. "Roughing it in the Bush." "Winter Camping II." But what about swimming or skiing? What about? What? We are solemn about our choices, our children, our diets, and our houses. Does one provide lunch for the workmen redoing the kitchen? Can divorce be a growth experience for the children? Husbands and wives discuss Male and Female relationships not with each other but with the man painting the living room or the twenty-year-old receptionist.

In the museum, the first statue to capture his attention was the head of the youth, but later it is the couple that he remembers. Again it is the vividness of contour and the smile(s) that captivate the eye. "Terracotta, 525 B.C. Cerveteri, the sarcophagus of the bride and groom," says the accompanying plaque, yet neither identification nor classification tells him anything of what the statues are.

Even the naming is an imposition, not knowledge. Etruscan is heard, read but not understood.

"This is the difference between us and the Etruscans: they believe. . . .

The statues fall forward when they fall.

Why?

Who knows. They fall forward; they are buried face down.

All of them?

Well not all. The Apollo of Veii was excavated standing up. But most fall forward. Noses, protuberances break.

Fragmented forever."

Numbing. George's hand was on his face, pushing and pulling for a response. But even when he dug his nails in there was none. Half of his face was alien flesh.

Julian was one of the few who was not embarrassed, who continued talking. Coolly, of course, ironically, if possible. Yet, here he was: beaming.

"You'll never guess who you have for a ward mate. I never expected. The people you meet. And here in Edmonton, yet."

"Ummm."

"The grandson of Alfred Z. My favourite painter. Of the last two hundred years anyway."

"Who?"

"That man I was talking to."

"Great." George began a description of the lady, the knight and the games. He meant it as a warning, but Julian responded with amusement and a touch of interest. George countered by overemphasizing the strangeness of the girl. He quoted "La Belle Dame." Julian smiled and lifted an eyebrow. George admitted he'd read the poem on the back of a record album. Then he had to explain to Julian who Marianne Faithfull was, both in her earlier pure folksy incarnation and her present black leather grit and cackle.

"George, you should know by now that I am not interested in pop ephemera."

"O.K. a small digression. I'm just saying I wouldn't trust him."

"He has a Ph.D."

"History?"

"Philosophy."

"Worse."

"Why? Like the rest of us, he couldn't get an academic job. You should be sympathetic. But the point is that he has recently inherited some paintings, as well as family letters."

"So?"

"You are being dense. He needs some help from someone who knows some art history. To go through what's there. Alfred Z. I can't get over it. My favourite painter. . . ."

"Your favourite. I thought. . . ."

"Always. I always felt this, this kinship with *fin de siècle* Vienna. And Z., his work is so eerie, so fantastic, so. . . ."

"Willed." The professor interjected smoothly. "Deliberate. A mind running riot. But what can one expect. There was no tradition of painting in Austria at that time."

Julian was openly irritated. "I know the history."

"Excuse me. I couldn't resist. When I heard you discussing Z. I saw the Vienna show last month." The professor paused as if waiting for a response. "At MOMA, in New York." Julian and George still said nothing. "And to hear Rolf is Z.'s grandson." His white, curiously hairless legs hung over the side of the bed. He lowered himself carefully to the stool and then the floor. "I shall listen to him more carefully this time."

"Quite a discovery." Julian leaned closer to George and lowered his voice. "If I'm not elbowed out."

"He's just lonely. It gets boring. And no one visits him."

"Rolf doesn't even like Z. While I have always admired. . . ."

"What's this always?"

"Denser and denser, George. This is an in, a possible in. These paintings and letters could mean a show, a catalogue, articles, a book."

"All this happened while I was asleep? Did he give you a proper interview or just decide that with your looks you had to be the right man?"

"He just offered to let me see the paintings, but it's a chance. I know it is. And I'll make the best of it."

A new beginning from a random meeting. George had felt beyond it: too shaped, too set; but then an inattentive moment in a bar and here he was. Not exactly beginning. Julian's voice was growing softer and softer. "I don't belong in trade. I should be, I thought I would be. . . ."

As Cynthia had thought she would be a ballerina. As George too had thought, in the summers after Rome working on the Etruscan site, he would be an archaeologist. If he had been born ten years earlier, before the number of jobs shrank and the competitors multiplied. If. Instead, he was stuck piling up the dust rather than excavating it.

"I've just never been interested in contemporary art:

minimalism, pop. . . ." He should tell Julian that now all beginnings would involve shattering. "Though some of these new neo-expressionists, now they do speak to me. That playing with the iconography of the past. They are too often needlessly vulgar, of course, and technically. . . ." But portentousness was not George's style. And if Julian didn't feel it, he didn't. "And all the old masters are already taken, chewed up and digested so to speak. But to find new material: new *old* material. . . ." A joke might do it, a pointed phrase, but it was all too difficult with half of his head hurting and the other half gone.

"Great. Terrific."

"Yes." Julian's eyes focused on George's face. He was already uncomfortably close, looming. "Yes." The unspoken expectation, the sense of nebulous demand was suddenly back, a rock between them.

"Julian. . . ."

"I can't stop thinking about our summer. Ever since you brought it up."

"I didn't bring it up. I mentioned it. That's all."

"You and me and Jackie. And I ruined it. I had to. . . ." He hadn't been drinking this time. The boozy undertone to his breath was not fresh but a sign of the previous day's excesses.

"Look, I have other things on my mind."

"Yet, there was something too inevitable about it. First the two of you and then she and I." George flipped his sheet up so his face was half covered but Julian forged on. "And the two of us: such friends. Fated one might say. And if so, useless to castigate oneself. Now the three of us in this hospital. . . ."

"Pardon?" George flipped down the sheet.

"And I in vigil for both of you. Inevitable. Yes. Jackie's up in obstetrics. You knew she was expecting? The labour was quite horrendous, twenty-six hours apparently. She finally delivered this morning. I was waiting to hear about her and about you, and I kept remembering so clearly, that sun, the inescapable heat and one moment I'd think I ruined it and the next I'd say no. . . ."

* * *

In the eighteenth century, neoclassical times, they patched up some of the statues: added marble arms, plaster of Paris noses.

But would they look right? Authentic?

With time.

So they'd seem whole again.

Only with time.

George closed his eyes to Julian's insistence, to the near promenade of nurses, interns and bored patients, shuffling yet one more time up and down the ward; he closed his eyes to the narrow clear tube stretching from his arm to the hanging bag, to the distorted reflection of his already distorted, purple, yellow and green face in the metal of the pole. He pulled his cushion up around his ears, shutting out the rattle of stretchers and machines coming and going, shutting out the voices, querulous and condescending, shutting out the farts, the burps, the laboured breathing, all the anonymous sounds of decay.

Time repairs?

Time weathers, stains, and pits the marble.

The form doesn't concern me. It's the smile that speaks. I appreciate the proportion, the plasticity of the limbs – all that, but the smile, the archaic smile of that long lost world touches, it does, it's almost physical; it touches me.

So that, when the next doctor came, he poked George in the ribs to get his attention. "You didn't answer." He had a thick Slavic accent of some sort and a prominent chin.

"Sorry, I. . . ."

"Let us see." He was reading the chart. "The vein tied up. The bleeding stopped. No more the problem. You go home."

"But I can't. . . ."

"It's done."

George waved at the intravenous. "I still. . . ."

"I call the nurse. You dress."

He did long for home. But he should be returned to himself before he went back. "I want to see *my* doctor."

"I call the nurse. She will unhook you. You dress." He was writing furiously though what it was hard to imagine. He had barely glanced at George.

"My doctor."

"Which my?" A good question. Did he mean his family's GP, the woman who admitted him, or the one who had operated on him the first time (no, not him), the second surgeon (or had he been also the first)? Which?

"I can't feel half my face, for God's sake."

"No need to shout, my good man, no need to shout."

My good man, indeed. "I want some answers. Now." Was he actually saying these things? He hated to be as scripted, as predictable, as the opposition.

"The nosebleeds. . . ."

"My face. When will the feeling come back? This isn't right. I come in with a nosebleed and suddenly my face is numb? There's malpractice here. And I should warn you: I am a lawyer."

The Slavic doctor was clutching George's chart to his chest, his eyes totally blank. One of the nurses was at his elbow, speaking quietly into his ear. They drew back to a corner of the ward, turning their backs to George.

"I went to get the nurse," the professor's voice was neutral, "when I saw that he wanted to eject you so prematurely from the care and concern of this institution." His face remained deadpan. "We got back just in time for the 'I am a lawyer.'"

"Don't remind me. . . . I mean thank you. Well, it sounds extreme, but someone screwed up and I'm suffering for it."

"Suffering? Surely the problem is the lack of feeling."

"Mentally. Mentally, I'm suffering. And they're withholding information. Obviously, they aren't even keeping the chart correctly."

"Are you implying," the professor thrust his bald head out farther from his hunched shoulders, "a cover up?"

George let a short bark of a laugh escape. The anger was retreating, weariness taking its place. "Speaking of which, what happened to the guy over there?" George nodded at the curtain drawn around the bed opposite his. "All of a sudden he had a bandage around his head."

"He insisted on getting up. He had to get home, he said. The nurse finally stood back and he toppled onto his head. Now he has a cracked skull."

"There's a message there somewhere."

Nurse and doctor were back, reinforced by a tiny, frizzy haired woman that he recognized as one of the doctors he'd seen in emergency a few days before. The three of them stared impassively down at him, a grim line at the foot of his bed.

"I want to know when. . . ."

"Dr. Baricevich didn't realize you had been operated on again today. You will be discharged tomorrow."

"But did the operation work? No one will tell me."

She smiled benignly. "The operation was successful. We have every reason to believe sensation will return to your face."

"When?"

"We can't say exactly when." She patted his foot. "But not to worry, it will happen."

"Not to worry. Look, a mistake was made. Why not admit it. I had a nosebleed, you. . . ."

She intensified the concern in her voice and facial expression.

"Well, when we consider what could have happened and how the nosebleed was a blessing in disguise."

"Meaning?"

She hesitated, shooting a glance at the other doctor. "A stroke." George was aware of a sudden calm, all his previous agitation was gone. "You probably – we must use the word 'probably,' it is impossible to know exactly – developed a small blood clot. Why we do not know. . . ." George was so calm that he wondered whether he would ever move again. His arms and legs were heavy, even the tips of his fingers were stone.

* * *

Touches you, she says. Listen Buster, I'm the one who touches you here. Umm, like that? Nice? Forget marble. You want physical. . . .

Stop, he says. Be serious. Just one more minute. . . . Off. I'm trying to say something about the archaic smile.

I am serious. I titillated you with my books, I exposed my mind to you: how much foreplay do you need anyway? I thought men. . . .

This is after-play; we already –

We did. Let go of my hands.

Let me finish: it's the Mona Lisa smile, of course. It suggests –

I can still use my toes.

Wholeness. Sophie! A harmony of selves.

And my tongue.

A wisdom. (Oh yes.) Of being.

You still want me . . . to stop?

No.

It's all material.

Ummm.

All in the material. The marble dictated that the mouth be shaped that way. No meaning to it at all.

But the Etruscan statues, the couple on the sarcophagus, they're made of terracotta.

The artists were imitating the Greek style.

I don't believe it.

I am supposed to be an expert.
I don't believe it.

For an Etruscan, the clouds collide in order to create lightning.

Me primitive man. Me want you back here now.
Back there? Really? Now?

As George waited for Cynthia to arrive for her promised evening visit, he imagined the various ways he could tell her what the doctor said. Though the words he used varied, in each scene he was casual, ironic while Cynthia, for he imagined her responses too, was variously horrified, melancholy, and dismissive. Yet, when she did finally arrive, he found he could not begin. There were only fifteen minutes left before visiting hours were over, and she burned up the minutes complaining about the snowstorm, the sidewalk that needed shoveling, a neighbour's child who had bitten Sara, and George's parents who were off on a guided tour to China and, as usual, not around when you needed them. George could have interrupted; she did punctuate her monologue with "but how do you feel?" or simply "sooo?" But the tightness in her mouth and around her eyes stopped him. He knew her concern and her frustration were there, underneath, but to demand a demonstration seemed a bit cruel, or, at least, risky.

She was worried enough, he guessed from the closed face, the wandering sentences. Worried enough: too worried. She was trying to show the appropriate amount of emotion, the expected response. Measured lives, theirs.

They had to be balanced, always balanced. She had to be loving mother and strong wife, even if the essential Cynthia was frightened or confused. Their marriage was an elaborate structure of demands, built up from the fragile base of their emotions. And most of the demands weren't even theirs. He was Daddy, the supporter and protector, Daddy, law writer and law follower, Daddy, citizen. Daddy –

Roles as they said in psychologese. Still, it was perhaps more to the point than the structure metaphor. You held a position too long, your attitudes hardened: petrification. But what choice did he have? He could keep moving and shifting the way Ted had: from a follower of Buddha to a follower of Rajneesh with Reich and Perls in between. Or Anne striding briskly through marriages and marathons – onwards, ever onwards – faster, faster – and better. She insisted it was better, always better. As did Ted. His face gaunt from fasting, his new orange clothes already hanging on his frame. Her body so hard, if you touched her you'd bounce off; and her face, just try saying a slack or silly phrase to that face.

No, with potential and promise gone, the only choices were the inessential ones: that not this, this not that. Taken solemnly, often with much thought, discussion, and reading. A ritual invocation of the household gods. That car, this lock, that bed.

Terracotta, cooked earth: shaped by hand.

Terracotta, cooked earth in the different colours of the earth: sand, buff, pale gold, peach, mauve, apricot orange, reddish orange, vermilion: deep red, strong red, blood red.

By touch, he knew, by touch.

Evidence such as burial inscriptions and tomb paintings point to the fact that Etruscan women were considered equal to Etruscan men. Women played at gymnastics, ran businesses, took part in the public life, and, most scandalous to the Greeks and Romans, reclined and ate with the men at feasts. Their position, so unusual in the ancient world, led to calumny against the Etruscans. Authors as different as Theopompus, Plautus, Horace and Aristotle believed that this egalitarianism pointed to Etruscan degeneracy and immorality. The women were obviously "common to all men," Theopompus claimed. Yet it is the number of individual couples (loving couples) arm in arm, or holding out their hands to one another that is notable in Etruscan art.

And later it is the couple that he remembers, that he returns to, that he wonders over. "Terracotta, 525 BC, Cerveteri, the Sarcophagus of the Bride and Groom." *The couple*, he thinks of the statues in that way: distinct, underlined.

The actual couple, of course, was reduced to dust centuries ago. This couple represents that particular man and woman. More precisely, these statues give shape to the idea of the specific couple through the material of terracotta. From the material to the idea to the material. Despite such distancing, who can ignore the gentleness of his hand on her shoulder, the vitality in both their eyes, the common yet separate stance. This is no empty form. This is a marriage shaped, defined, and tender. Radiantly tender. Well might they smile.

Ahha! she says.

Ahha? he says.

Now I know why you're obsessed with those statues.

You do.

I do. Here you are presenting your interest as a fascination with the wisdom of the past. Dignifying it with theories.

What have I done?

Sit up. No, hold that expression. Look over there. See.

It's awfully dark.

I'll open the shutters a crack.

I'm grinning.

The archaic smile. Admit it.

I never knew.

And your eyes. Wrong colour but still. And the curve of your cheekbones.

I'm embarrassed.

You're not the first. A linguist from Tuscany has a book on how traces of Etruscan (an unknown language right) survives in Tuscan pronunciation. Then there's the Jewish historian who proved that the Etruscans were Semites and the Italians who insist they didn't come from the East at all but were indigenous. The Greeks. . . .

O.K. Enough.

Oh, and D'Annunzio –

Fascist.

Exactly. He thought the Etruscan's message was that life is basically anxiety and fatality while –

Sophie, I understood after your first example.

Contradictory fables springing from the same evidence.

Different readings but I still think –

Yes?

Eighteen years old. His first time away from family and home and in that first isolation, in that first lack of connection to the parade of sights, of tastes, of sensations, an intoxicating freedom. He had invented a new self in and out of that eternal sun. He presented himself as he wished to be and now was. In the cool dimness of the tombs. In the half light of Sophie's shuttered room. He'd had girls before (in the backseat, and once, difficult to imagine now, in the front seat of his Volkswagen bug, on the sofa in the rumpus room or even, when his parents were out in the country, on his narrow bed), but she was his first woman, those times together in Rome his first affair, not fooling around, not doing "it" but making love. Varied, inventive, and discreet love. She had insisted that they could not be open: she could be fired if it was known that she dallied with students.

"This is dallying?"

"Of course not."

"With students?"

"You know what I mean. It's what it would seem, from the outside."

And he had acquiesced at the time. They rarely sat next to each other at meals, they faded away from the group at separate times, she wouldn't even look at him at the dig. George hated that most of all. His eyes were drawn; he couldn't help it. She looked so right in khaki shorts and white T-shirt, so tanned and strong and long-legged.

"I could stare at you all day."

"Such gallantry."

"You'd be surprised."

She did move to another pensione, where no one from the group was staying, so he could come unobserved on the odd siesta break or late at night. He never said anything to Julian. He thought Julian guessed who he was with those nights he wasn't in his bed. Sophie did occasionally join the two of them and Jackie on an expedition or an evening of wine and talk. And the one time she came to his room Julian had answered her knock. She stood at the door looking embarrassed and upset, and Julian had glanced at George in a way that had seemed knowing and then excused himself. "Jackie's waiting." Instead, all along, Julian had thought Jackie was the woman. After Sophie ended the relationship, there was no outward sign it had ever existed. No one else knew. Sophie didn't want to remember. And George tried not to.

So why now?

Pursued by broken limbs, shapes from another time.

After so many years?

A hole in the nose, a hole in the knowing and not knowing.

* * *

Early the next morning, the professor was informed by the ward nurse that he was being moved to a private room. "The tests must have turned up something," he told George.

"Nothing serious, I hope."

"I suspect so." He was fussing with his top sheet, smoothing it out. "I'm at that age."

"You're not that old."

"Middle age, I meant: children almost grown, separated from wife, six or seven years till retirement. Everything slipping away."

George was embarrassed. He wanted to offer some wise words "Buck up, you still have – " blank but could think of nothing to fill that blank. "It doesn't have to be like that."

"Doesn't it?" The professor was suddenly amused. "You think you'll be any different in twenty years?"

Rolf was already gone, either discharged or moved, George wasn't sure which. He had made lots of noise going: loud goodbyes, long jargon-filled explanations of his condition, but George hadn't paid attention. Rolf's replacement was young, still in his teens. He had a large blond mustache and a certain swagger. He was dressed, of course, in a hospital gown, but it was easy to imagine him in tight jeans, a work shirt (cigarettes bulging) and a trucker's hat. Shit, he kept saying, or hot dooggee. He was telling a story to the now subdued boy in the bed opposite. It involved two women, cunt number one and cunt number two, a case of the clap, a night of drinking, a fall from a balcony and his kidneys. "The doc says. . . ." Every now and then, he would look over at George and nod, as if to acknowledge him as a fellow man of the world. You know, the nod said, these things happen.

It was time to make a move. George was cautious. Although he edged himself off the bed, when he stood, the floor lurched, the walls shifted. He waited until all was still, then adjusted his gown and pulled on the flimsy robe. He felt exposed; the robe and gown skimmed his knees and he was very aware of his bare buttocks. There must be no falling. At least he wasn't hooked up anymore. He'd hated trundling himself and the metal apparatus. Clomp. The hospital slippers flapped on his feet. Clomp. Clomp. He nodded to the silent, head-bandaged boy, then the wattle-necked old man by the door. When he moved his head, his scalp felt as if it were attached only on his forehead, as if there were an inch of air between his brain and his hair.

He wouldn't hold onto the wall. He'd concentrate. No glancing in at the private rooms. No pausing before the nursing stations. The corridor was full of sounds: the intercom paging doctors, the television sets blaring, but his footsteps and his breathing echoed ever louder. Careful. Slow but steady. Dept of Nuclear Medicine, Radiology, Urology, Rheumatology, so many parts to the human body that can go wrong, breakdown. Watch the wall. Through the doors. One floor down. Over and over, his hand to his cheek, no longer a search for sensation but a habit, almost a tic. A long glass passageway, two more corridors and finally the women's pavilion.

He paused for a moment's rest, threw a glance at the mural by the elevator and then looked again. It was a fresco of the Alberta landscape: prairie, foothills, and mountains. In the foreground, an Amazonian-sized pioneer woman was staring fearlessly into the future. She was wearing the traditional costume, but one shoulder and one breast were bare. She was woman holding her babe to her breast, woman clear-eyed and clear-browed, facing the future.

"Can I help you?" The woman at the information desk was eyeing his bare legs. Two flower-laden men got off the elevator. They also stared at his legs. The smell in this section was different, the undertones acidic rather than bitter, animal rather than chemical.

The halls here were busier. George had to dodge several clusters of visitors, besides numerous shapeless women (in fuzzy or shiny polyester housecoats) and the odd abandoned stretcher. He began checking room numbers although he knew he wasn't quite there. This was still miscarriage and hysterectomy territory.

Another station, nurses chatting about some movie, did they ever do anything but talk to each other? The usual crowd around the nursery window. George stopped; he couldn't help it. He'd spent so long staring through that window, joyfully at Michael and more ambiguously at the twins, that his response was habitual. An ugly bunch this one: all wrinkled faces and swollen heads. But then, though he and Cynthia had found Sara, Jane, and Michael perfectly beautiful as newborns, perhaps a non-doting eye could have found fault. When they re-looked at pictures of those first weeks, the children did look odd, not half as cute as they were now. Their vision had been determined biologically; they were new parents. But what is not determined? Wherein do we think and choose? There is no choice of gender, class, culture, or age? Especially age. The terrible twos, the balky fours, sulky adolescence, carefree twenties, responsible thirties, it just went on and on. And time? How to think outside of the moment.

Do events have a meaning because they have happened or do they happen in order to express a meaning?

2266. The door was half open. George knocked and, without waiting, entered. The first bed was mussed but empty. Jackie was sitting with her baby on the other. She was obviously startled to see him. She gazed blankly at him, her breast out. And only when he drew a chair up to bed and sat gratefully down did she, with a quick, fussy gesture, pull the top of her nightgown up and then smile.

"My goodness, George."

"Jackie, how's it going?" He was rather startled himself. He had been expecting the old familiar Jackie, not this slatternly woman with tangled hair, lumpy body, and tired, tired face.

"I heard you'd been beaten up, but I didn't think. . . ."

"Julian's been up here too, has he? Talkative boy, that Julian. I didn't get beaten up. Doctors did most of the damage."

"Oh, do look at her. Isn't she gorgeous? I just can't believe that she's here. That I have her, after all those years of. . . ."

"Gorgeous. . . . Got your eyes."

"Do you think so? She's got Mummy's eyes, poor little thing, Mummy's eyes." The sudden spurt of animation, the abrupt switch to an arch tone, these were familiar: remnants of the old Jackie. "She's so stubborn. I just can't believe it. She won't nurse properly. She won't. Either chews, Christ it hurts, or she gets this set stubborn expression. Now my nipples are cracked. You can't imagine. . . ."

"You should talk to Cynthia."

"Right, anyone who can nurse twins." Jackie continued the baby, nursing, labour, and delivery talk, talk that embarrassed George but which he encouraged nevertheless. (He was a courteous man.) The baby twisted itself about in Jackie's hands. She offered an engorged, blue-veined breast; the baby began to squawk; she tried massaging its cheek and then moved it to the other breast. George went to get a bottle of sugared water from the nursery. Once the rubber nipple was wedged through the baby's lips, it began, contentedly, to suck.

"Rejected again."

"It takes time."

"What do you know?"

"Well. I do have. . . ."

"I can't do this. I'm too old to start."

He patted the part of her body closest to him, her knee. "This is just a stage. Feeling like this. It passes." She shook her head, her eyes full of tears. "Just wait. In a day or two. . . . And you're not alone. There's Alan."

"Sure." She shook her head again. Her hands on the bottle and the baby were steady but her face contorted.

Not another teary, George thought, just my luck. "It'll be fine. You'll be fine, better than fine – terrific." Unconsciously, he had fallen into the soothing tone he used on the children.

She jerked her knee away from him, sat straight up, and thrust the baby with bottle at him. By the time he had adjusted the squirming bundle and blanket, so that it lay comfortably in his arms and he was gazing into its ageless infant eyes, Jackie had locked herself in the washroom. "You really should talk to Cynthia," George shouted at the door.

The baby let out a squawk. Awkwardly he rearranged it against his shoulder and began to pace the small room.

"Brings back memories," he said to the wall. (The feel of a tiny body in his hands, the almost inhuman sound of a newborn's cry, he had forgotten much.) "You'll be surprised how fast it goes." Then he remembered Cynthia's words: "I mean, it seems eternal at the time, but then, boom, they're on to the next stage."

"Pardon me." A pretty young woman in a bright pink housecoat with matching cheeks and lips had entered while his back was to the hall door. She arranged herself on the other bed, fanning out the bottom of her housecoat, undoing the top button. "You a relative of Jackie's?" Her smile was amused, knowing. Her fingers were busily fluffing out bottle blond hair.

"Friend. Old friend."

"Another one, eh? Well, she needs y'all. Keeps turning on the waterworks. I keep telling her. Leave the kid in the nursery. Try some formula. We'll be stuck with them soon enough. But she's read too many damn books. Bullshit experts. I'm one of – "

The washroom door opened. Jackie had washed her face, tied her hair back with a ribbon, and drawn her characteristic dark lines around her eyes. " – six and my Mom always said – " Jackie held out her hands for the baby. " – the watched flower – " Her expression still solemn, she lay it down in its cradle.

"Shouldn't you be getting back. The nurses will send out a search party."

"I doubt it."

"Yeah, what you in for? Though I got my suspicions." Pretty in Pink seemed as determined to keep him there as Jackie was to have him leave.

"It did start with a fight."

"He-man, eh?" Pink's smile managed to convey yet another level to her knowingness.

"It's time for baby's bath." Jackie insisted, although the

baby had fallen asleep.

"I was completely innocent. Just sitting drinking my beer." George found himself sitting on the edge of Pink's bed.

Jackie was standing just behind him, speaking almost in his ear. "And April, weren't you going to that exercise class?"

"Gotta work on the old abs. Why don't you come? You could use – "

"I need my rest."

"Look Jackie. It won't take long, honest, but I have to talk to you about something else. Just a couple of minutes."

Jackie looked at him and then nodded. "I know."

But, after April left and he and Jackie took up their former positions, she sitting up in bed, he in the chair by the bed, he realized he didn't know how to begin. The part of his face that he could feel hurt and he was suddenly conscious of how tired he was.

It was Jackie who broke the silence. "I'm sorry. I just hate for you to see me like this."

"Come on. We're old friends. And you've just been through a rough time."

"'*Old Friends. Set on the,*' is it sofa or shelf ? '*Set on the sofa like bookends.*' No, that's not it. I always liked the melancholy in that song."

"Julian did come up and talk to you yesterday."

She stopped humming. "He talked at me. I was even more out of things yesterday, as you can imagine."

"I've been remembering that summer in Rome. I mentioned it and he started going on and on." George stopped. Her head was turned, her eyes fixed on the cradle. "Right, talking at me. He has a weird version of things. He must have been saying the same things to you." George stopped again.

"So?" She spoke softly.

"Well, he's wrong."

"So, what are you waiting for me to say?"

"Well, this stuff about, about my being in love with you and you choosing him over me."

"Yes?"

"It wasn't like that."

"Yes, I see." Her head sank back onto her pillow and her eyes closed. "You certainly were not in love with me then or any time after. If anyone was pursuing anyone, it was me you. Finally I gave up, turned to Julian. You want me to tell him."

"No. . . . I just wanted – "

"What? What is the point now. I mean, who cares. Besides Julian, of course . . . it has been a long time."

"I wanted the past to be clear."

"Clear? If it's that." And she shrugged. "Anyway, if we're playing truth or consequences, why did you hang around so much?" She stopped, shook her head. "Anything else I can do for you?" This directness and impatience was new. George was tempted to label it postpartum prickliness. He would have thrown the phrase at the old Jackie, and she would have laughed. But he couldn't say it to the woman before him.

"No. It's just. . . . We are good friends. We got that out of those days. That summer." He stopped.

Then she had been as oblique as George. And he had found it restful, a pleasant change, that lack of taking things head on. No expectations. "Look, George, out with it. I can't read your mind."

Out of the sun, in the dimness of his shuttered room. Sweating from the heat. From Sophie's touch. Each place her body meets his, pools appear. Her head is turned to one side on his pillow. A tear marks her profile. Rivulets, streams. They are not flowing with this river but riding it out. (Ease off, yes, a bit more to the left, hold back, hold.) And afterwards, she gets out of his bed, "we're swimming," and stretches out on Julian's. She faces George as she talks, the top part of her body propped up on an elbow. In the gloom her damp skin glows like marble. He wants to speak, to answer, but his mouth is puckered, his tongue numb with the taste of salt.

"I was involved with someone else." He stared down at the baby as he said it.

"I had an inkling. Girl at home, I'd say to myself. Though, hey, I know I'm very resistible."

"Sophie."

"Sophie. . . . Of course. But why are you telling me this? I can see you discussing it with Cynthia but –"

"It seemed right. You were our cover before and after."

"Fine. I understand. Your point has been made. I was used from beginning to end. You can go. The past is clear. Sordid but clear. Part of it anyway. You know George, I didn't need this now. Not at all."

"I'm sorry."

"I didn't need it. I don't need it. Why don't you go? You just keep sitting there, staring at me. Why doesn't a nurse come? or April? No one's ever around when you need them."

"Please, Jackie. You'll wake the baby. I didn't mean to. . . . We did, after all, become friends. You know I think the world of you. . . . Look, Sophie didn't want anyone to know. And then when her fiancé turned up, I understood why. I didn't want her to know how badly I felt." His words did seem to register. At least, as he spoke, the colour faded from her cheeks. She leaned back on her pillows and again closed her eyes.

"You wanted her." Her words came in a tone so casual that, what with her closed eyes and somnolent expression, they seemed to come not from her but through her. "I wanted you, or thought I wanted you, and Julian thought he wanted me. A – common – story." Her words floated out of her mouth and up, up to the ceiling.

"And if, underneath, you did want me a little bit and Julian didn't want me but you, that's also a common – "

Did she actually say those words or had they sounded only in his mind? "Pardon," he said.

"There's always another layer," she said.

That her face, at first just ghostly
Turned ©

He knew he should go. He had managed to say what he came to say. Still, the exchange seemed incomplete, and he felt confused, even deprived. He sat watching her face, waiting for a further phrase or a sign, waiting to sense that the long ambiguity between them was over. But Jackie did not speak or even open her eyes. He intended a dignified exit: a kiss on the forehead and a gentle phrase, but as he stood, the ceiling lifted then plunged.

She said, "There is no reason
and the truth is plain to see" ©

So that in the years to come when he looked back on that time of the nosebleed (his phrase) often the first image he would remember was this: his sitting in Jackie's room his head down between his knees.

* * *

John appeared while George was waiting for Cynthia to arrive and take him home. When George had given her the news of his imminent release, she had said nothing for a moment. When she did speak, her voice was shaky. He could feel the intensity of her relief. She was finally showing how worried she had been. Yet, she complained when George insisted that she and not Julian pick him up. "I'll have to get a sitter. This may take a while." George was sitting on the end of his bed, dressed and ready to go. The boy from the bed opposite, no longer howling or comatose, was sitting on George's chair but speaking to Rolf's replacement, the youth with the big blond mustache. The boy's speech was a sequence of mumbles and twitches. (George could only decipher a few words "Man . . . Fred . . . stuff . . . baby.") John seemed amazed by the boy; he stared at him pointedly. Or maybe he was amazed that the chair was taken.

He stood awkwardly at the foot of George's bed. "Ready to go, eh? Finally. My timing's off, that's for sure." In his dark brown three-piece suit, John seemed to stick out in a way the other visitors to the ward hadn't. "You still don't look great." His very blandness, viewed separately from Bob's, was aggressive: his hair, clothes and bodily shape so neat, his features so tidy.

"Guess you've learned your lesson. Eh, George? Stay out of the bar. Look, let me give you a ride home."

"Cynthia's coming."

"I'll give her a call; save her the trip."

"I'm sure she's left by now."

"Need to talk. Let me try and call."

"You can talk here." John made a show of looking round so George added, "We can go to the smoking room."

"It's not that important or anything," John said when

68

they got to the room and through all the usual questions about George's health. "I just thought that being we're friends and all I should tell you."

George knew he was expected to express interest and encouragement. Instead he kept his eyes on the television.

"Warn you so to speak," John said, "so you'll be prepared when you come back to work."

"Not till next week, I won't be back till then."

"Bob said you felt Blanfield-Jones' job was yours."

"He did, did he?" On the television, a string of severe looking models were striding up and down a ramp. The clothes were all dark and voluminous; the models flipped and swirled their skirts as they strode.

"Well, it seems that actually the job's his, Bob's I mean."

"Knows already, does he?"

"Not officially, of course, but. . . ." John said.

The camera zoomed in on the face of one of the models. She held her chin out at an odd angle. The word STYLE wrote itself in red across her haughty mouth and eyes. "You know it doesn't matter to me."

"Pardon?"

George turned from the set and looked into John's eyes. "I don't care. Bob's welcome to it."

The bruises on his face turned purple, yellow, and green and then faded. His strength came back quickly, before the bruises were even gone. Within a week he was back at the gym running his laps and lifting the usual weights. But the feeling in the left side of his face did not return. He could smile, frown, lift an eyebrow; his face performed on cue, but the flesh remained numb. The doctors continued to speak of patience and of giving it time. George shrugged and waited. He was not ready for resignation.

It's all in the tone
he told Cynthia
in the tone
arguing for Willie Nelson. George had taken to playing his albums whenever the children let him displace Sharon, Lois and Bram. Cynthia was scornful, "Mozart, Handel, Mahler even. Please."

Well, maybe not just the tone. The phrasing. Definitely the phrasing.

For, listening to Nelson sing, George suspected that it hadn't been just the song that had brought back Rome. The difference in tone, the pretensions and intensity of the remembered original contrasted with Nelson's irony and regret, had also worked on George, reminding him of the past and the passing of time.

"Middle age," he said.

"Speak for yourself," she said, as if it were easy.

And more and more, the only way he could speak to her was with his body. By touch.

It was not his fingers, though testing his numb cheek was a habitual gesture now, but hers, a casual caress, that first brought forth the trace of a sensation.

Another known, unknowable alphabet.

He lifts her hand to his mouth. He leaves a circle of kisses on her palm. He tongues each juncture of the fingers. He proceeds up her arm, catching blouse and flesh gently between his teeth.

The habit of tenderness.

For a moment, when she lies naked and waiting and he still stands, he sees not his marriage bed but the narrow bed of the pensione, not Cynthia but Sophie, sly peppery Sophie, young, unmarked Sophie stretched out for him. The illusion is brief; the touch of Cynthia's leg against his banishes it. Still, Sophie survives as seasoning, salt and pepper. Man and woman, George and Cynthia.

Skin to skin   soft   tongue to tongue   soft   habitual softer familiar softest love.

The couple, husband and wife, are half lying, half sitting on their bed. Their hands are open, speaking.
    She is smiling.

        He is smiling.

It is a moment of completion, of impenetrability to all that is not he and she, a moment of both reading and understanding. And then, the moment is shattered by a howl.

    "Sara."
    "I think its Michael."
    "Anyway, its your turn."
    "Mine! I was up half the night last night."
    "Your memory's defective. That was the night before last."
    "He'll wake up the others."
    "*Your* turn."

ACKNOWLEDGEMENTS

The publisher and author gratefully acknowledge the following for permissions to reprint quoted material:

From *A Whiter Shade of Pale,* words and music by Keith Reid and Gary Brooker. Copyright © 1967 Westminster Music Ltd., London, England.

Seferis, George; *Collected Poems 1924-1955.* Copyright © 1967 by Princeton University Press. Reprinted by permission of Princeton University Press.

"Boney Fingers"
Lyrics and Music by Renée Armand and Hoyt Axton. Copyright © 1974 Irving Music, Inc. & Lady Jane Music (BMI). All Rights Reserved.   International Copyright Secured.

Every effort has been made to obtain permission for quoted materials. If there is an omission or error the author and publisher would be grateful to be so informed.

Becoming Emma

A special thanks to Kay Stewart and Gary Watson
who both read and commented on the first draft
of *Becoming Emma* and with whom
I discussed the informing ideas.

A thank you also to Alberto Severini who helped
me to understand genetic research.

Weave me into red-white-red
Weave me into our flag
Andrejs Eglitis

Personal style must be added to the style of the school, the country, the race.
Heinrich Wofflin,
Principles of Art History

The double root of style.

A painting. A figurative study of a woman. She is sitting on a brown chair, her elbows on a table, her blonde head bowed, her hands half-covering her face. Light from a window crosses the canvas in a diagonal slash, over the table strewn with speckled dishes, a tipped box of cereal, a spilled clot of jam. Her clothes are dark, her face obscured by her hair. The eye is drawn to the vertical line of her pale arms, vulnerable and bare in the cold, bluish light.

I

She was an expatriate, an American, who had lived in Canada for years. She did not stand out in the neighbourhood where she and her family lived. It was close to the university and thickly settled with faculty. On her block alone there were three other wives (one British, one Indian and one other American) who were in Edmonton only because their husbands found the research and financial inducements the university offered them too tempting to refuse. She did not, as the others did, complain loudly and bitterly about the climate, the landscape, or the culture and character of Canadians in general and Albertans in particular. She was quick to volunteer for duty days at the neighbourhood play school, quick to smile when you met her in the park, even if the words that accompanied the smile were often sharp or ambiguous, quick to accept or give invitations for coffee. She was a tall, slim-hipped woman: friendly, forthright – American, the other women agreed, from the tip of her ash blonde hair to her penny loafer clad toes.

For years, Emma was also (both sides of the have-a-career versus stay-at-home split agreed) a devoted if overly indulgent mother, driving her boys to lessons and plays and concerts, playing with them, actually down-on-her-knees *playing* with them in the park, at home, if you dropped in. Then, a year or two after the birth of her third child, she began to change.

INTERRUPTION

Think of your progress around the contemporary art section of a museum. Your eye is caught by a large, but unfamiliar, canvas. You pause, give it a quick once over, and then, before any further consideration, you check out the accompanying plaque. Often the name of the painter is familiar and then you think, of course, Jackson Pollock, abstract expressionist. You have been given a clue, a category, a way of seeing what is before you. You might not consciously recall what you have read about his work and the movement, but your mind might throw up phrases, explanations – "the dissolution of the pictorial into sheer texture, into . . . sheer sensations. . . ."

The title of the work can be a further clue, particularly if you are not an avid reader of art theory. The plaque says Ellsworth Kelly – *Two Oranges and a Green*, and the painting consists, indeed, of two squares on the white canvas, each in a different shade of bright orange, with a bright green square in between. Form, you think, and colour. That's all – all and everything. And your companion, if you are with a companion, as I have been, who is a little less receptive than you, will say "cheerful, I guess."

Or you are staring at a Mirô – all red and blue colour patches and wide black lines – and you think you see the outline of a cock and balls, but before you mention it your companion says "hey, tits and an ass." So, you turn to the plaque: *Dawn Perfumed by a Shower of Gold.* "Quite a metaphor," your companion says, "didn't Zeus come down once as a shower of gold?" Or "What about that fairy tale you told me about the bad sister that was showered with tar and the good one with gold?" while you remember the definition of the term in *The Happy Hooker*. Should you explain? You glance around the room to see if any other gallery goers might overhear you.

"Nothing so heavenly," you begin. "We're talking dirt here. . . ."

Together you decide it is a joke, a big joke in pretty colours. Though if you see the painting again, or think later, you may decide that like the balls that could be breasts, the title both obscene and ethereal does point the way.

The title of this story is *Becoming Emma*. It could have been, for many months it was, called *The Closing of Emma's Mind*, a title with certain connotations, certain echoes. For this is partly the story of Emma's education, her American education. But it is also about what happened because of that education; it is also about how Emma became Emma.

Terra Marriana, Livonia, Livland, Courland, Letgallia, Lettland, and the Latvian Soviet Socialist Republic: these are the names that foreign invaders have imposed on Latvia.

When Emma was born, her parents had named her Aida after her maternal grandmother, who had been killed a few years earlier by a Soviet bomb. As a child, as soon as she reached the point of self-consciousness, she was not enthusiatic about her name. Aida, it was too heavy, too serious. But she didn't decide to change it until she was thirteen. She and her parents had just moved from Brooklyn to Glen Falls in upstate New York. Her father had a new job, his first job in America as an engineer. They had a new house, so new that parts of it were still unfinished and her father spent many late nights and weekends painting, applying baseboards or tiles. She was about to enter a new school in this new town, a picture perfect place of curving streets lined with Victorian mansions and trees. She felt as if she was beginning a new life, a life closer to that of the families on television: an American life in a way that her life in Brooklyn was not. For, despite her categorization by her neighbours in Edmonton, as a child she never felt American. (And was not really to feel it until she moved to Canada.)

In fact, the whole family had only recently been naturalized. And though she had, of course, been pledging allegiance to the flag in school for years, at the moment when she swore to renounce her *country of origin* she felt a tremor of illegality and when hand on heart she pledged allegiance to the republic of the United States of America, promising to protect and defend it, she felt as if she was both telling the truth and pretending, that to be naturalized was somehow unnatural. Yet, becoming a citizen was what she wanted, what they all three wanted. It was the next step in the process by which they were being transformed from free floating specks, blown here and there, at the mercy of the winds of chance, into something settled, rooted, a natural part of the landscape. (Or so her father's theory went.) And the citizenship did bring her father security clearance which, in turn, together with American accreditation, brought this new job, the first one, after ten years of working on assembly lines and as a janitor, that was appropriate to his education.

It wasn't as if she had a nationality to renounce. She had been born in Germany in 1949, but as the daughter of refugees, she did not merit German citizenship. She was officially a *displaced person*, her passport issued by the United Nations. Displaced, *removed from her proper place*, a place she had never seen and that no longer was shown on a map. When anyone asked, as they often did, "So, where you from?" her father would answer, "We came from Latvia, tragic Latvia, violated Latvia, and now we are here. Americans, the great melting pot, yes?" But at home he would repeat, "We are always, in our hearts, always Latvians." And her mother would say, "The country lives; not there, here: Latvia."

> Weave me into red-white-red
> Weave me into our flag

Otherwise, neither parent was prone to melodramatic utterances. At first, they took her name change calmly. Her father laughed. Her mother lit another cigarette.

"I'm tired of having everyone mispronounce it," Aida said.

"So, you're going to change it? You're being illogical again, *meitin*," her father said, smiling.

"All the kids make fun of it. Laugh at me."

"Children will find a way to make fun of any name, any one," her mother said exhaling smoke and tiredness. "It's better that you learn to deal with it now. You'll be facing worse."

"More idiots. I can guarantee it. The world's full of them," her father said, still smiling.

"It's like I'm named after an opera. A particularly dumb one where they have horses and camels onstage." (They had seen a production at the Met the year before.)

"The pronunciation is not the same."

"I know that, Mother. But the spelling is."

"And I know that."

"It's as if you thought I would grow up to be a two-hundred pound warbler. Or a slave girl even. Rather than me."

"We did think you'd grow up to be celestial, Angel. Look at it this way – at least we didn't name you Desdemona. Did I ever – "

"Yes."

"Tell you about the man who named his first son Othello, his – "

"Daddy, thousands of times."

In preindustrial times, her professor told her, there was high culture and folk culture. Now there is the avant-garde and kitsch.

At first, Aida named herself Sandra. A week before the move, Aida and her best friend Velga, another one of your Balts – as Velga put it – went twice to see a movie they both adored. It was called *If a Man Answers*, and it starred Sandra Dee and Bobby Darin as newlyweds who didn't get along until Sandra decided to follow the advice from a how-to-house-train your dog book in handling Bobby. The rules of puppy training turned out to be more than useful in husband training. She soon had him "eating out of her hand." Both of these adolescent girls realized the movie was light comedy, a humorous comment on, rather than a guide to, male-female relationships. Still, the idea of a system, presenting itself just at the moment when the male species had suddenly become a mystery and a prize, was alluring, particularly to Velga.

"It's all in knowing how to manage them; I'm sure of it," she said after the second viewing. They were sitting on the stoop outside Velga's apartment building, eating double fudge ice cream cones and discussing the boys they knew, especially one who was older, wilder, with tighter black jeans, bulkier muscles and darker eyes than the others.

"Italian eyes," Aida said, sinking her teeth into the scoop and the cone. She let out a muffled "eek" as the cold hit her gums.

"Bedroom eyes." Velga countered between dainty licks.

"What! Velga, what are you saying? How do you know? What do you mean?"

"You know." Another tiny lick.

"But. You think he? He *is* crazy. I can't even talk to him. I get all shaky."

Velga was cool. "As I said, it's all in the management – of yourself, of him. Control."

Aida was not convinced. Her mother was an intelligent and, when judged against the other mothers, a glamourous woman, but she had no control over Aida's father. The family revolved around him, his comfort, his wishes and his enthusiasms. If there was a simple system, surely her mother would know it. Unless it was her pride, unless she knew and scorned to use her knowledge. Aida could believe that. "I don't know. I think it works for Sandra Dee because she is Sandra Dee. She's . . . she's all sweet and cute."

And in her observation of the boys at her school or her father's friends or even the shopkeepers around the neighbourhood, she saw them respond to Sandra-like qualities in women, to sweetness, cuteness, softness. Sandra, the name summed up the aura, all fluffy and pink, that drew men's attention. Aida had the same haircolour as the actress and the same pink and white skin, but the rest of her was disappointingly different. Already, Aida was tall, broad-shouldered, with sharp cheekbones, deep-set eyes and a long, narrow nose. What else could she expect with a name like Aida Avendemis? What else would anyone expect? If at least she had a turned-up nose, she was sure her whole face would look better: softer, rounder. It was no use bringing up the idea of plastic surgery with her parents. They would laugh and, if pressed, insist she was too young. For now she was stuck with her nose and her face. But her name – she had more control there.

She was registered at her new school as Aida Avendemis, but on the first day of class she told the teacher and the other students that her real name, her "Christian" name, was Sandra. This had worked for a girl in her class in Brooklyn (her official name was Jung Woo, but she had everyone call her by her Christian name, Theresa) and it worked for her. Everyone accepted Aida as Sandra and everyone called her Sandra. Everyone except her parents.

They continued in their insensitivity. Her mother would quietly correct any friend phoning for Sandra. Her father threatened to expose her fooling, as he put it, to her teacher at the parent-teachers' night. Aida adopted a plan of passive resistance. She refused to answer or respond in any way when they called her Aida. They tried yelling or cajoling; she acted as if she were deaf. Her father would put his mouth right up to her ear, "Aida, baby, please," and she wouldn't even blink. Her mother capitulated first. She began referring to her simply as "hey, you." Her father continued to alternate yet another repetition of the glorious history and significance of her name with passages of sarcasm which he thought of as wit.

Until, one Sunday morning, after eggs, bacon and pancakes, her mother said. "I'm so bored with both of you. This has to stop." She tapped her ash onto the remains of her pancakes.

"Both of us. What are you saying – both of us?" her father said. "I wish you wouldn't do that. There's an ashtray right here."

"Both of you. Boring." She scattered more ash on her plate.

"If you would just call me Sandra." Aida kept her voice quiet and firm.

"Boring."

"Aida, you're going to your room for a week if you keep this up," said her father.

"Enough. Look, what if we all compromise?"

"We call her Aidra?"

Her mother put a hand on Aida's wrist. "You can be

called whatever damn name you want – Brigitte Bardot, for all I care at this point."

"But. . . ." Her father was spluttering.

"Let me finish. Any name at school or with friends. But at home your real name is your name. With no complaints."

"No more smart-aleckness," her father said, anxious to be part of the solution.

It was not long afterwards that Aida, to her embarrassment, began to suspect that as a name Sandra was a poor choice. She tried to explain to Velga who had come from New York so they could spend the last days of their Christmas holiday together. "The weird part is that at first it felt right. Well, not right but sort of neat. And then, it didn't. It isn't me. I thought I could become a Sandra, but now I don't think I can."

"Sandra Dee lost her magic?" Velga suggested.

Aida shook her head. "I just realized the magic wasn't going to work for me." She didn't want to admit to Velga the combination of trivialities that highlighted the gulf between herself and the name: the two Sandras in her class, one dark, one blonde, but both petite, cute, and advertisements for what the name should represent, together with one of her father's comments, one that she disputed hotly, that Sandra sounded Russian. (After all, wasn't it short for Alessandra?)

Velga had followed her friend's lead and renamed herself. Then, in adjustment and acceptance, she had taken the lead. She was Marianne, totally Marianne. "I was never a Velga. Never."

"Lucky you." Aida said, thinking nothing is ever simple for me.

"Come on, you just chose the wrong name. You're not doomed to be Aida. Choose again – but the right name this time."

"And make a fool of myself? Scrub Sandra, put in – "

"Lookit, I didn't change school or place and I managed it."

"But I'm not you."

The history of Latvia from the beginning of the thirteenth century until the end of World War I is the story of conquest, subjugation and domination of the Latvian people by foreign powers.

Sillers, *Latvia*

Folklore is superficial, said another of her professors. You must look to where you are going, not from where you come.

When they still lived in Brooklyn her parents frequently had friends over for the evening. Their small apartment was the unofficial centre of a certain circle of Latvian exiles. Many of them had known each other in Riga before the war. Most of them had been studying at the university. Then they were the children of the middle class: comfortably, comfortably preparing themselves for their proper future. Without a thought, they'd been sure of who they were, of what was theirs. They had been aware, who was not, of the clouds on the horizon. They'd prepared for rain, a hailstorm, not the deluge. Now they were out of place, insecure, confused, but dogmatic. All was reversed: what was, was gone; settled youth flipped into an adolescent middle age.

88

Now, like teenagers, they talked and speculated and argued through the long nights. From the moment Aida opened the door the words would spill out, a week's worth of hoarded words pouring out over her head, sometimes delicately trickling down her cheeks. The men bore bottles of vodka and cognac. The women carried baskets of *piragi*, buns filled with bacon and onion, or potato salad with beets and herring into the apartment already fierce with the sweetsour smell of slowcooking sauerkraut and caraway. Liquid words, Latvian words: "you must never give up your language," an older cousin would tell Aida. The tumblers were already out, waiting. The first bottle uncorked.

"My grandfather always said, no opened bottle in the house," her father said each time he poured. "Drink up."

When there were other children, she played with them in whatever space could be found – under the table, in a recessed corner, in the middle of the kitchen floor. "This is our house." She snatched almonds from the top of the saffron yellow *klingeris* cake, or passed out hard, herbal candy to her substitute family. "You be sister. I'll be Mum." Over their heads, another bottle was uncorked. "I won't be baby this time." Her mouth puckered with the pungent sweetness. English on her tongue, sleepiness in her eyes. The adults' words thickened, solidified. They fell like stones around the make-believe house.

When there were no children, she watched and listened longer, usually from a visitor's lap. Some conversations were repetitive: whether the Latvian Council, based as it was on pre-war members of parliament, should still be allowed to speak for all Latvians; the quality of one or the other production of an opera in Riga in 1936; the probability of the U.S. supporting with troops any attempt to recapture the homeland; the perfidity of the Russians; the treachery of the Germans and the vulgarity of the

Americans. These, as well as cards, quickly tired her, weighing down her eyelids.

But, if she managed to stay awake long enough, (something that became easier and more important to her as she grew older), the words changed again. The grown ups almost never talked of the war. And only within the family were the names of the dead pronounced. But, late in the evening, letters were brought out and passed around with the vodka and the cigarettes. Each one of the letters had been tampered with: opened and scrutinized and then reglued with coarse paste, censor's paste. A sort of guessing game would begin. What was not being written? What had been written, but was subsequently cut? Was a line such as "but we told you about the grain harvest in our last letter" a code? Or had there actually been such a letter that was confiscated? How much of the latest package, that'd cost so much to send, had been received? Had the coffee, sugar, and stockings arrived and been considered not worthy of comment? Or were they stowed away in some Russian's larder? If an uncle or a sister was not mentioned, did it mean nothing, an oversight, or was it a sign of imprisonment or exile? And those who had been taken away: had they been executed? tortured? starved? Were they dead, dying, or merely suffering? Under scrutiny, the phrases and words that were left on the almost transparent paper lost their fixedness.

One of the men would begin to sing a folk song. Someone else would join in.

> Here is Kurzeme
> Here is Vidzeme
> Here Latgale

Velga's mother would tell a joke, yet another counterpoint. One of the younger men draped, while laughing, his arm around her shoulder. Aida's mother got up suddenly from the table and, her eyes watery, went off to the bedroom. Aida's father and a friend still argued over the tone in which to read a sentence. Aida hoped there would be no sudden shouted words, no sharp angry gestures.

> Fortune decide our fate
> Guard our land
> One soul, one country, ours

Auntie Anna knocked over a half-full glass. The song trailed off. Velga's mother was crying now, showily, white handkerchief in hand. Two fresh voices took up the melody again.

The lyrics floated over the noise.

Words
clouds   smoke
ink-smeared paper
sweet powder cologne   sauerkraut   vodka breath

air   dreams.

Now there is no folk culture, only the ersatz, only kitsch.

Clement Greenberg

About a year before the family moved from Brooklyn, the parties began to diminish in frequency. Her parents seemed to be losing their taste for company and chaos. Her mother often made their father phone and cancel the evening an hour or two before it was expected to begin, using a migraine as an excuse. Aida was not sure if the process had been gradual or sudden, but she knew that, just as she had grown more and more frustrated with her name, she'd grown bored with the parties, that she was repelled by the words and gestures she'd been hearing and seeing all her life. The allure of the late evenings, those peepholes onto the complex of adult life, was gone. When Cousin Andris, trying to prove his strength, lifted her father and staggered into the stove, she didn't find it funny. When she came upon Velga's father shaking his wife (between the toilet and the tub in the bathroom), she responded no longer with alert interest but with disgust. It was sordid, too sordid, and she did not want it to touch her.

The tone of the parties had grown more frenetic. The years were passing; exile no longer seemed temporary. Alcohol and regrets swelled, then inflamed formerly innocuous actions and emotions into deformities.

It was the time of Adolf Eichmann's trial. The newspapers, the magazines, even the television shows were filled with the horror. What had been done? A man in the U.S., a Latvian who lived in Houston, had been accused of complicity in the murder of Jews in Riga. But the accusation came from Russia, the information from the KGB. None of the guests discussed the case. No one knew the man. But the Russians would do anything, they all agreed, anything, to defeat the last nationalist. What was a little forgery to them? Or a faked photograph? Smeared ink. A cluster of grey dots. Smoke. "So how can we know," Cousin Andris would ask, "how can we know?"

Aida began to keep herself aloof from the parties. She would take Velga, or any other child that she was forced to entertain, to her room to chat or play a board game. If there were no other children, or only infants, she holed up alone with a book, ginger ale, and pretzels.

She had graduated from Nancy Drew and Trixie Belden to what she thought of as very serious and informative historical romances with plucky heroines, arrogant heroes, dastardly villains, and tempestuous "love." "Bodice rippers" she later learned they were called. When the ripped bodices, heaving breasts, multitudinous ringlets and long searching kisses palled, she moved on to the more subdued Regency romances of Georgette Heyer and these led her, in her search for more of the same, to the novels of Jane Austen. So, like many of us, it was through an imitation, by way of a distortion, that she came to the real.

The Avant Garde imitates the processes of art; kitsch imitates its effects.

Aida read the novels, all six of them, the way she watched the Sandra Dee movie. They were full of hints of how life should be lived; be good, they said, and you will be rewarded with "perfect happiness." Grow in understanding and principles. Avoid idleness, ignorance, and meanness. Do this and your garden will be cultivated, your prospect pleasing, your house an elegant mansion. How more effective than the costume romances was this as a bulwark against all that was happening outside her door. In Austen's world, moral choices were important; they had consequences. Words had meanings, shared and agreed to meanings. Words were what they were supposed to be – words. They did not metamorphose into stones or liquid or even air. You read them and you knew them.

Outside Aida's door on those party nights, in the kitchen and living room and hall, was a wilderness where Aida knew little and felt much. Outside was confusion and loss, outside was a murky connection between black and white magazine photos of stacked corpses and sepia-toned family portraits, a grey link between the good old days and terror. The grown-ups argued whether Nazism or Stalinism was worse. Aida heard – there are no reasons, no choices, no consequences. The innocent and the wicked were both slaughtered.

She heard and she read until the words on the page ate up those in the air. Emma. Elizabeth. Catherine. Marianne. Elinor. Fanny. Anne. Elizabeth was her favourite. But she felt more like Emma. The sounds and the emphasis were close to her old name. This was America, the promised land, a cultivated garden in a white picket fence of good fortune. And she was an heiress to her parents' hopes and expectations. In the upstate town, Aida chose to be Emma and looked about her for a Mr. Knightly to instruct and guide her.

It was only many years later in Edmonton that she realized how appropriate the name she had chosen for herself was. This is the story of how Aida became Emma. But, as she came to see, her model was not the fortunate, pampered Emma Woodhouse, but the other one, the more universal and pathetic Emma Bovary.

II

But despite repeated material destruction, unmerciful plunder, deadly plagues and frequent humiliating defeats by a succession of foreign invaders, the Latvians have managed to survive with their cultural identity intact.

Sillers, *Latvia*

Now there is no folk culture, only the ersatz, only kitsch.

Clement Greenberg

A few months before Emma began to change, before she began to show signs of exasperation with the roles of good neighbour and supermom, she came to a realization. She was bored. She counted her blessings: children, husband, self, all healthy, all whole. But, of course, that changed nothing. She was busy, every moment of the day, busy. Michael, her youngest, had learned how to walk and climb, and, if she relaxed a moment, he would be somewhere he shouldn't be, scattering garbage, unscrewing the top of a bleach bottle, pulling apart his brother Harry's newly-made model airplane.

When she was first married, before the boys, she'd sewn herself some elegant outfits. She could start again. She bought cotton for a simple sleeveless dress. She stayed up late to cut it out. But then for weeks the pieces lay untouched on her sewing machine. She never had more than ten or twelve minutes at a time before she was interrupted. A row of stitches and, inevitably, a distant scream. What now? Not again? When the dress was finally finished, the hem sagged, and the neckline didn't lie flat. She threw it in the garbage.

Her situation, she knew, was a common one for a mother of young children: busyness, interruptions. And even more common was that old, familiar female curse – boredom.

INTERRUPTION

At the beginning of both their stories, her namesakes, the Emmas (Woodhouse and Bovary), are bored, dangerously bored. Enclosed in her house, Emma Woodhouse sits alone with her father, "in mournful thought." It is the evening after the wedding of Miss Taylor, her governess and companion; Emma is only too aware of the long October and November evenings she must "struggle through" without anyone or anything to cheer her. In her narrower, more constricted house in Tostes, Emma Bovary gazes out of her window, longing both to die and to live in Paris, while her husband trots around the countryside. Desperate, Madame Bovary is reduced to speaking to her greyhound. "She would have confided in the logs in the fireplace, or the pendulum of the clock." Her boredom is a prison; she sees her life as a long, dark tunnel with a closed door at the end.

Emma first read *Madame Bovary* at college for a course. She was not as taken up, as convinced, by Flaubert as she had been by Austen. She accepted her professor's pronouncements on Flaubert's greatness. She wrote a paper on the symbolism of fog and water. But though she could imagine herself wearing the heroine's gowns (saffron silk) or, delicious thought, seduced in a horse-drawn carriage (round and round the town) she could not, as she did with Emma Woodhouse, identify with Emma Bovary. She found her too foolish, too flaky: most unlikeable. She agreed with the American publisher who described Madame Bovary as "that girl who behaved badly."

Her next reading of the book came around the time of Michael's birth. She had set herself a schedule of masterpieces, partly to combat the torpor of pregnancy, but she could not keep to it. She found it hard to concentrate. One page and she was asleep. So she began and then rejected various works: *Moby Dick, War and Peace*. But the first few pages of *Madame Bovary* managed to catch her interest. She was at Charles and Emma's country wedding when her waters broke. She took the book with her to the hospital. Between the contractions, for hours they were fifteen minutes apart, she read. Afterwards, she read when the house was quiet during the night feedings. Once Michael had latched onto her breast, she would use her free hand to hold the yellowing paperback (it was her college copy), balancing it a little on his bald head.

This reading left her with a confused memory of the master work. Some sections she forgot completely, while other scenes stuck with her as if she had lived through them, as if she had merged with the French heroine. In particular, she remembered certain details with almost hallucinatory intensity: the sickening scent of the basket of apricots that Rodolphe sends Emma Bovary to break things off, the hissing sound her corset string makes when she impatiently pulls on it; and her extended death agony, after she knows she is ruined and has ruined her husband and child and takes arsenic, the thirst, the nausea, the shrieks, the convulsions. With almost hallucinatory intensity, yet coloured by what Emma was experiencing as she was reading, by her physical sensations. So some of the details were tinged with pain, and others were suffused with the sweetness, the vulnerability, she felt breastfeeding Michael.

The arctic front hung on: a glacial tooth and claw, a weight pressing down on everything and everyone, slowing down cars and people until creaky, brittle, they threatened to break, to stop. No wind, only cold, no air, only ice on the lashes, in the lungs. Ten, twenty, thirty below zero. Cover up, Emma ordered the boys, wrap up. It's dangerous out there. Where's your hat, scarf, boot? Not again. Not another one lost? Be careful. Take care. Your fingers could drop off. It's forty below. Frost bites.

Andrejs glanced furtively at his hands. Harry rolled his eyes. Oh, Mum. But the words sprang from her fear and leapt out of her mouth. Frost bites.

Thirty, twenty, see Mum, it's not so bad now, ten below. Zero. Emma hurried out to do her chores, to take the boys tobogganing, to check out a sale. The edges of the snow were softening. Puddles collected on the sidewalks, in the road. Then, snap, a new cold front, so now there was a hard layer of ice beneath the snow. It was even more difficult to walk outside. Frances's husband, Jerome, had slipped on his back step and fallen so hard that he broke his femur in a spiral fracture. He'd needed a steel rod from knee to hip.

It was treacherous out there. Emma wandered from room to room in her house. Room to room. Ice crept up the windows. Run away. Cold pushed at the doors. Run away. Shriveling the plants. Run away. Buffeting the walls. Run away. Reaching for her. Run away. Room to room. Her thoughts froze into the shape of the furniture, into piles of laundry and scattered toys. Her body grew numb. Inch by inch.

Sleepy by day, awake at night, she climbed in and out of bed. Juris grumbled. How could he sleep with her flip, sigh, flip, sigh? She watched late night talk shows. She walked through the darkened rooms. She started letters;

she read magazines. Now and then she attacked the kitchen or a bathroom, scrubbing away until the fumes of Pinesol brought Juris and his please, Emma, have a heart. And, abuzz with wifely virtue, she would retreat to the basement to start sorting the wash. But in two or three days the boys were complaining again they had nothing to wear. The soap scum on the sink, the coating of grey ash, the yellow stains on the toilet base were back. It's all up to me, she'd shout. All of it. You're messy. You're careless. And, worst of all, you're ungrateful. Every one of you.

After an outburst, they would all promise to change. Juris would assign chores: Harry sets table, Andrejs sweeps, Michael clears, Dad does dishes. But after a few days they would lose energy, forgetting or finding excuses. She would nag. Andrejs would argue. Harry would insist he was helping; he was remounting and ordering his butterfly collection. Juris would suddenly be at a crisis point in his experiments and forced to spend extra long hours in the lab. And Michael, well he was still so close to babyhood. The battle was still hers. Endlessly hers. Juris never understood how bored, how tired of it she was. Every day. Dust, dirt, mold. Every day.

She wanted to be away, run away, from it all. Run away, but how? Run away, but where? Anywhere but here. Run away. If she thought she could run to another place, any place but here, this house, these rooms – dusty, chaotic rooms. But she saw no path from here to there. Only trackless snow. Only sheer ice.

Besides she was hooked, hung up on the wall with her feet dangling, by her feelings for her boys and for, yes, Juris, hooked under the breast bone. To wiggle free would rip her apart. The love of a mother, the love of a wife – how sweet it sounded, how soft. But, for Emma, it was elemental: blood warm and metal cold.

The boys' fights grew noisier and nastier. Me first. I get the bigger piece. It's mine. I had it first. That hurt. Duffous. Dummy. Dork. Poo-brain. Out of my face. Until Emma would screech or throw a book, or, more and more often, go off to her bedroom, close her door and lie down, leaving them to slug it out. You want to draw a little blood. Would that make you happy?

Mom's losing it, Andrejs told Harry. But she had already lost parts of herself, parts of who she was. Frost bitten. The flesh grows numb. It turns white as snow, then hard and blue as ice. Thirty, forty below zero. Below nothing, below a circle circumscribing an absence. Emptiness. No, a minus, a negative capability cancelling the positive.

Boom.

The stone itself was special: limestone that came from Germany.

The ritual

had to be performed exactly right. She began by carrying the stone to the basin. There she ground off the last image. She drew her design and covered it with gum arabic. Then, she took her bottle of acid and spread it over the surface. She had to be careful. She had to be exact. Too little and she would be left with nothing; too much and she would also be left with nothing. It was a question of balance – the right balance. She wet the stone. She rolled on the ink. She was sensitive to how the ink was pooling, to how the stone was absorbing. She was aware. She put on a wet piece of paper. She put on blankets and wax to get the stone through the press. She was careful. She was exact. Too little pressure and there would be no printing; too much and the stone would break. Awareness, balance, always balance.

Frances was at the door, ringing and knocking. Emma stood motionless at the window. "I know you're there," Francis was shouting. "I need to talk to you."

Michael emerged from the kitchen, robot in hand, and without a glance at his mother, he crossed the living room to the entrance. Emma heard the front door unlock and open. She heard Frances stamping off snow, babbling to Michael. Then, she was there – "Just thought I'd pop round" – looking her usual utilitarian self.

"Not a good day," Emma said.

"I can tell." Frances was visibly taking note of the state of the room. She even picked up a couple of the strewn shopping bags from yesterday's trip to the January sales and placed them together, neat and tidy, in a corner. "Find any bargains? I never venture into Mr. Donovan's or June's myself. Much too dear for me. But. . . ."

"Go away, Frances." That pulled her short.

"I only came to pick up Michael for a little visit. Ian's in the car. Get your coat on, Michael. They can play for a couple of hours."

"They don't like each other very much."

"What do you mean?"

"I wanna go, Mum. Honest."

"Then, go." Emma said. "You want me to pick him up?"

"Don't worry. I'll drive him back."

"What's up? Did Juris talk to you?"

Frances hesitated before answering. "I ran into him the other night at the skating rink."

"You have your own husband to take care of."

A flush spread over Frances' sharp features. "You should pull yourself together. For the children."

"Gather up the pieces?"

"Get some help then. Juris mentioned you've refused to see anyone. He's at his wit's end," Francis said, as if Emma didn't know.

Received Ideas, Edmonton 1988 version
Get a job.
Get a life.
Take a pill.

What's wrong, he'd ask over and over. And when she shook her head, he would examine her with the type of attention he gave one of his cell lines. He was used to mysteries, that was what he did, he'd say, solve mysteries, but he believed in standard methods of procedure – formulating a hypothesis or two and designing some experiments to test the hypotheses. Let's investigate some alternatives, he said. If this depression is chemical, he said, and perhaps even genetic, medication is the solution. Go see Duke. It's worth a try. Get a prescription.

A prescription, she said. "Is there such a thing? A magic potion that will turn the negative into the positive, turn absence into presence. Is there? I didn't know. I hadn't heard."

"I can't talk to you anymore. Please, Emma . . . I want to see you happy again." And he did, because he loved her, and also because her state was complicating his life. It was inconvenient: if she didn't pay attention to home and family, he had to, and that ended up disrupting his work. He had his class to teach, his lab to run, the deadline for his grant application was approaching.

Please. One evening she broke half the dishes in the kitchen; a rampage which began innocently enough, a dish slipped from her hand and the sound was so satisfying, so right, that she kept on, from the draining board and around the sink, one after another, cups, saucers, bowls, plates crashing against the far wall, against the floor. She walked over the splinters back and forth, crying, scrunch, scrunch, while Juris tried to sweep up. Please, he said, please. It can't go on. So, she gave in, it couldn't go on, she went to the doctor, who was eager to prescribe. Take them myself.

"Now I'm tired and numb. But better. In other's eyes. Manageable," she told Janie, whom she hadn't seen in awhile. "All the edges are off."

"If those are your only side effects, you're doing well," Janie said.

"Have you taken them?" Emma refilled Janie's coffee cup.

"Me? No. I run." She stretched out her scrawny body on the chair, resting her hand with the cup on her jeaned hip. "Compulsively, fifty miles a week. . . . Endorphins do it for me."

"I have bad knees."

"Anyways, Beatrice down the street, when she went on anti-depressants, half her hair fell out. Frances got a terrible rash."

"Frances? Not our chin-up, let's-shoulder-on Frances?"

"Believe me, Frances. Been taking them for years. And Ines, she turned into this edgy bundle of nerves. I saw this show on "Donahue," some people who aren't suicidal, get suicidal once they start."

"I didn't know it was so common. I guess I should take comfort from that. I'm not unusual."

"Listen, half the women on this block . . . probably half the women in Belgravia are on something. . . . Prozac fiends. Lithium junkies. What's the statistical chance that they all have a chemical imbalance?"

"You don't approve."

"Me? Whatever gets you through. It just bothers me that it's the women who are being medicated. After all these years of feminism. It's the women who need the pills. Whether they're out working or at home. Something must be very wrong."

"It's winter, it's boredom, it's the place, all our failed expectations."

"Sure – life, nasty, brutish and short, as they say. There are lots of problems, but why only this one solution?" Janie shook her head. "I have a friend who's one of the most balanced people I know. She's had a tough life. Her parents died and then her first child. The next one was born severely handicapped. She's weathered it all with . . . with courage and grace. The first time she started to waver, to have problems managing, the first time, she was on medication. Just like that."

"We have to manage. That's our role – managing. Keeping it all going." Emma laughed. "We're being turned into the Stepford wives."

"Help," Janie said.

"Help," Emma said, still smiling.

Received Ideas, Edmonton 1988
Women have choices.
You can be anyone you want to be (even if it's only for fifteen minutes).
Women don't have choices. In this patriarchal society, they are victims.

Still longing to get away. The emptiness, that negative space, could only be assuaged, filled, elsewhere, there not here. And her elsewhere, her other place, was a bubble in her brain, a fantasy world, a dream of possibilities that she sometimes confused with an actual city. New York. She read *New York* magazine and *The New Yorker* every week, cover to cover, including the "Sales and Bargains" at the end of the former and the "Goings on About Town" at the beginning of the latter.

NAME THAT TUNIC – about 200 one of a kind couture samples are discounted here. All come in narrow cut sizes of 4, 6, and 8. *Wesley Brown, Fay Chiang, Mary Gordon, Oscar Hijuelos and others talk about how writers' ethnic backgrounds affect their work. No ticket necessary.* Black silk-crepe dinner suit with white pique trim, retail $1,800, here $680; *March 5: Fred Schneider, of the B-52's, talks about his career.* Ivory metallic bustier dress with gold metallic cocoon wrap, retail $1,750, here $650; *Alan Shields – Paintings on canvas embroidered with patterns of black, white, and coloured threads. The pieces are very optical with touches of orphic futurism, Op art, and Tantric art, as well as the mysticism of Alfred Jensen and the ritualistic, somewhat zany informality of Alighiero e Boetti. Through March 2* . . . amethyst silk gown. . . .

She read the magazine, the Arts and the book review sections of the weekend *New York Times,* as well as the monthly *Interview* for the downtown scene. When she was feeling clear-headed and energetic, she waded through the more confusing *Art Forum.* She knew what was hot, what was happenin': the pulse, the rhythm and the rhyme of the city. She knew which restaurants to eat at and which to be seen at. She knew the play to see, the gallery to visit, where to go dancing at two or three in the morning.

New York: she longed for the woman she could be there. Elegant, compassionate – caught by a camera flash entering the AIDS benefit at the Metropolitan Museum. Critical, superior – caught leaving the opening of Julian Schnabel's latest show, whispering in Hilton Kramer's ear, it's all hype, all empty gesture, I see no substance. Ironic, informed – caught mixing with the crowd at the BAM opening of another new four-hour Robert Wilson/Philip Glass opera, debating whether it was artistically necessary for him to use Sanskrit yet again, I mean give me a break, puuleease.

INTERRUPTION

As I worry over the commonness, the everydayness of Emma's life and fantasies, I remember how Austen said that in Emma Woodhouse she had created a heroine no one but herself could like. But the fact that she did like the self-centred girl is important.

How different were Flaubert's feeling towards his heroine. He complained that he suffered writing *Madame Bovary*. The banality, the vulgarity of his characters nauseated and disgusted him. He would have preferred to write another "Oriental Tale," full of exoticism and violence. He had already spent three years working on *The Temptation of St. Anthony*, but when he read it aloud to his closest friends they urged him to burn it at once. They condemned it as lacking in originality and style, and as too confessional. They told him he must learn from Balzac and turn to realism. After his Oriental journey, Louis Bouilhet gave him the plot for *Madame Bovary*. If he hadn't been pushed, told that it would be good for his writing, Flaubert never would have chosen a subject he found so mediocre, unglamourous, and commonplace. As a nine-year-old, he wrote to his friend that he would note the silly things a lady who visited said. From adolescence onwards he collected Received Ideas *(idées reçues)*, envisioning a Dictionary which would so discredit clichés that everyone would be afraid to open their mouths. And he had to spend five years with characters who spoke and thought only in preconceived ideas. Five years. Revolting! How he suffered.

How arrogant, I think, how cold, to separate yourself from people in such a way, to judge from such a perceived feeling of superiority. I watch my Emma, but not from above. I know that stupidities often flow from my mouth, though I hope less frequently from my pen. I know that Emmas are not just around us, reader. Emma, *c'est nous*.

Still longing. She was like a hungry woman craving a meal; the emptiness, the need and the longing were one. Yet, Emma had had a good education. She was self-conscious. She knew that her dream was too small or, at least, too partial a thing. What had she envisioned for herself all those years ago when she was an undergraduate? Life in New York, certainly, but because it was to be life at the service of Art. High Art. High American Art.

That was what her education prepared her for. To be at the centre, at the pulse of American culture. After all, this was not the nineteenth century, an amiable, indulgent governess (à la Miss Taylor) or a French convent school plus heavy doses of romantic novels was no longer considered enough. This Emma had been given more than lessons in drawing and music and needlework. Though she had actually been sent to those lessons too. Her parents were ambitious for their only daughter. She was to have all the old, European accomplishments, as well as the best of American educations, the very, very best. For a woman.

Not that her parents could have given her the best, which, after all, was beyond the reach of such relatively recent (and honest) immigrants, no matter how fast they were integrating, if chance hadn't presented them with a particular opportunity. Emma was in grade eleven at the time pulling in good but not spectacular grades. She was distracted by what she was learning at the hands (and tip of the tongue) of her new and first steady, Frankie, an incarnation of her old taste for the cool and the muscular. If asked, she would shrug and say she thought she'd try a campus of NYU. Her parents would cluck, her mother groan in her theatrical way, "What do you have in mind?" Emma would say in her best adolescent whine, "Can you really see me at Harvard?"

Then the opportunity: her father applied for and got a job managing the physical plant on the campus of one of the Seven Sisters. They were moving to Connecticut, away from Frankie and to, as her Dad said, serious academe. Emma wailed she couldn't move again; she had her life, she had Frankie, her parents were too mean. This is the American way, her father told her, you move to get ahead, you move out and up. At least, the choice now is ours, he said. Not mine, Emma said. Not mine. Though once they were in Connecticut, she put Frankie behind her soon enough, probably because, before she even left, he had moved on (and down) to a girl with a beehive hairdo who cashiered at K-Mart.

She picked up the idea of the woman's college and after one look at the campus, ivy on golden granite, laughing, energetic girls, an enormous library, a good small museum and three Henry Moore sculptures on the quad, held it close to her heart. Her grades shot up; tuition fees were waived for the children of staff. She was in. Auden, Lowell, Mailer, Vonnegut. Pinter, Albee, Ellsworth Kelly, Motherwell, de Kooning. All the best, that is, all those considered the best in the late sixties in the Eastern U.S., came through, spoke, read or gave workshops. Emma took a course in photography taught by Walker Evans. She studied poetry with John Berryman.

The seriousness, the exaltation of high-minded art, enlightenment through the realities of light and space, filled her and her classmates. They floated through the bright globe of art, past and present. The highlights of history as a set of visuals.

Arrayed just for them. All the best: high art, high society. Emma was learning the language of art criticism, the language of classification and aesthetic judgement. Emma was being educated in the signals of status, another level of categories and evaluations. Her classmates were the daughters of the rich and the established. They arrived trailing cars and pet horses. Their clothes, depending on their major, were either discrete and expensive, the definition of preppie, or flamboyant and probably French.

Class suddenly mattered. When Emma felt out of place, it was not because of her Latvian background. In fact, being Latvian seemed beside the point, inessential, a costume reserved for holidays. Here another set of differences counted. She learned to dissemble, to camouflage. Luckily, art students were expected to be a bit different, conforming to New York art world, rather than campus, standards. Emma wore head-to-toe black, which obscured much discount store cheapness. She stopped referring to the facts of her life, to Brooklyn or immigration or parents. She cultivated reticence, imagining herself mysterious. And she worked hard: she would know what there was to know. She was young enough and American enough to think that with the proper education and dedication she could be whatever she wanted to be. Hadn't she slipped into the elite already? Semesters of reading, studying, drawing, painting. Semesters of dreaming, hoping. She drew herself a blueprint of a converted New York studio/loft. Wasn't she already in?

The artist is an existential matador fighting in the arena of the empty canvas.

Harold Rosenberg

Action painting is not 'personal' though its subject manner is the artist's individual possibilities.

Harold Rosenberg

In 1940, 78 percent of the population of Latvia was Latvian. In 1979, 53.7 percent was.

"A nightmare. It's become a living nightmare. I never go to New York anymore. Believe me." Emma's mother, Laila, had arrived with various New York bought presents.

"You have an odd idea of never," Emma said, examining the scientific game for Andrejs from the Museum of Natural History. The night before she'd been overjoyed to see her mother. Today, she found her physical presence – the ladylike way she sat on her chair, her hands folded on the table, her resigned facial expression, her sweet perfume – irritating. Laila pulled out her package of True cigarettes from a pocket in her skirt. "Mum! Come on. You know I'm not going to let you smoke in here."

"I came because I was asked."

"What can I say. Juris panics easily these days." Emma's mother lit her cigarette. The bend of her head, the click of her lighter spoke – take that. "Mother! . . . O.K. Sit by the window. Open it a bit more. But later, when it warms up, you sit outside."

"There are other things I could be doing, more interesting things."

"I'm sure."

Emma poured them both another cup of coffee. Her hands shook ever so slightly. As the day passed and she would drink cup after cup of her thick boiled coffee, the trembling would grow worse. But she couldn't give it up or even cut down. She needed caffeine, she told Juris, to get her through. She often didn't feel like eating, and usually coffee and toast was the only thing she could force down. She got up and put a slice of bread in the toaster. "Want some Mum?"

"I ate my breakfast at the normal time." She was watching Emma through the smoke. "Aida – you left the bag open. The bread will dry out."

Emma's chest felt tight, constricted. "It's already dry."

Laila's face was expressing progressive levels of reproach. She sighed loudily, showily. "I do know what it's like."

She was offering Emma a new kinship, the possibility of understanding. "Talk to me," she said in Latvian. It was a gift to be valued, but Emma could not hold out her hand, could not take it. She remembered too well her mother closed in her bedroom for weeks on end. "It's her nerves again," her father would say. "She needs rest." And once, or was it twice, visiting her in the hospital, her face a yellowish white, under her eyes plum-coloured circles, her voice a lifeless whisper. "Aida, baby." I bet it's your fault, Emma thought, I bet I got it from you.

But she said to her mother, "It's like bringing coals to Newcastle, you coming now to see me."

"Selling iceboxes to Eskimos. At least, I had my reasons." Answering her English with Latvian.

"What do you mean by that?" Emma's chest was actually hurting it was so tight.

"Juris adores you. He told me; he wants whatever you want." Emma made an irritated gesture. "Wait, your father and I, we gave you . . . everything we could. All your life, you've been handed everything possible on a platter. . . . And you . . . you waste it."

"Ah, you came looking for gratitude. Oh, what a lucky girl I am. Lucky and appreciative. To my special husband. To my wonderful, if depressed, mother."

"I lost my country. Everything I was. And it wasn't so easy for me, not like your father, to find myself here. Nothing's been easy for me."

"I know. I know. Look, Mum, with me – Well, I'm like

an old lithograph stone. The old picture has been ground away. And a new one hasn't yet been drawn."

"Very clever. But what about the boys?"

"What about them?"

"They need more than a blank stone."

Emma's mouth was suddenly full of saliva. But she did not speak. She swallowed her anger, leaned across the table and picked from a pile of art show catalogues, her mother's gift to her, the bottom book. The ones that had been on top fell over onto a dirty mug and dish. Emma did not react. She opened the book at random and began to page through the colour plates. The mother let out another one of her loud sighs and then, when Emma did not move or speak, she remade the pile. "Emma," she said. The daughter did not look up from the art book; her only answer was a slight toss of the head. "Emma, you know your father and I are most distressed that you have given up speaking Latvian to the boys. But since I've arrived, I've been struck even more about what a sad situation it is. Michael doesn't seem to understand me at all. Andrejs is down to a few words. Harijs. . . ."

"It's useless."

"After all, we taught you, Latvian school every Saturday. . . ."

"I told you, when Andrejs took so long to start talking, the doctor said his exposure to two languages would complicate things."

"Nonsense. Such doctors! Our country has been destroyed. It is our duty to preserve what we can. And the language – that's the basis for everything."

"We live in North America. The boys will never have a reason to speak Latvian. If they ever do go over for a visit, which I very much doubt, it will be like visiting any other foreign place."

"Never."

"Besides, with present trends, no one there will be speaking it either. Come on, Mum, you know the numbers are shrinking every day."

"Precisely my point. But don't speak of "present trends." Don't speak as if you accept what's happening. It's deliberate – deliberate genocide, their Russification."

"I've heard all this before, Mum. I know."

"And yet you willingly turn your back on your language."

"Sorrowfully rather than willingly. It's no use, is what I'm saying. I can feel as guilty as you want. But I can't turn back the tide. Not me. And what if I do insist the boys learn? They'll be able to function in a narrow ethnic ghetto. That's all."

"I can't believe what I'm hearing. You always said. . . . When you married Juris, you seemed dedicated. . . ."

"It seemed more important when his mother was alive. You know what her English was like. And she had this big family pride thing since her father compiled that dictionary."

"Of course. Think of the history of Juris's family. Do it for them if you won't for me. Keep the idea alive."

"If I thought it would mean anything. . . . It's been forty years since the war. It's time to face facts. Doomed is doomed." Not wanting to see her mother's pained expression, Emma had continued to flip pages throughout the argument. Suddenly, she paused, brought the book closer to her eyes, and screamed. "It's mine! It's my lithograph. Mine. And no acknowledgement."

Received Ideas, Connecticut 1969
Tune in, turn on, drop out.
Go with the flow.
Formalism ensures quality.
Never trust anyone over thirty.
Art should be about itself, nothing else.

In the summer after her third year of college, Emma was chosen to work with and for the famous Jack Nadow during the two weeks he was to be artist in residence on the campus. Emma was ecstatic. Jack Nadow had been tagged, certified by the best of New York critics as important, original, brilliant, a painter's painter, an abstract painter's abstract painter (though it was not until years later in Edmonton that she heard Greenberg call him "the greatest colourist in the History of Art"). This was her chance – not just to rub elbows with greatness – there had been plenty of that during her time at the college; all her childhood roughness (dry patches of ignorance) had been rubbed off by those well oiled interchanges – but to assist, to partake of that sacred quality.

Jack Nadow wanted to experiment with prints, silkscreens, and lithographs. The college was making available the equipment and a technician. The printmaking professor had picked Emma from the throng of eager applicants, because, he said, you're serious and you're good, praise that was particularly sweet since he had showered her with negative comments for two years. Clumsy, he would say, rhythmless. It doesn't work; it can't work, no. Emma would bend her head and listen and, unlike some of the others, would never argue back. Yes, she would say, I see, she would say, impassive as a rock. Then, she would go home and find that she couldn't eat supper, and when later her father brought up a tray, when she started the toast and tomato soup, the hardness in her stomach softened and she started to cry. Her father, as usual, cracked a joke, one from his standard repertoire. She yelled at him to get out of her room, leave her alone. He would begin a Latvian tale, often a story of a poor kind girl and Mother Luck, or the poor brother and Bad Luck, drawing it out, adding pedantic footnotes so that he would never quite reach the end, which she knew anyway: the poor grew rich, the good girl married the prince and the bad girl burned to a crisp. Stop with the tales, she would say to her father. Still, soon she'd be sniffing and eating, soothed by Campbell's and white bread.

For she loved working in the printmaking studio more than anything else. Here ideas, skill, and intuitions all fused. Stone, water, wax, acid – each step involved care and balance. Ink, water, paper, press – she spent much of her spare time, evenings and weekends, working, chatting with the other students. Try another kind of wax crayon. How about the darker grey stone? Is the image sharper? More resonant? Oriental silk fibre paper or heavy handmade French? This or that? Mastering the art.

Now she was going to work with Jack Nadow. The first day as she waited for him in the unusually quiet studio (the other regulars having been exiled for the duration), she paced – past the sinks and the presses, past the shelves of acids, inks, and rollers, back and forth by the wall of windows. Her left eyelid had an almost invisible quiver, an outward sign of a deeper, inner tremor. The famous man was late. She wondered if she could turn on the radio and fill the silence. But then what station should she choose? The classical one? Or would that seem pretentious? She felt like top forty pop, but to turn that on would make it seem like she had taken possession of the studio, making it her space. *Wild thing*, she sang to herself,

. . . my heart sing. She took up position at the farthest window from the door, pushing her face almost to the pane, peering out at a large maple tree, trying to focus, to really see one individual leaf.

Until finally he was there, led in by the professor. Emma was overwhelmed with waves of embarrassment: the way they caught her – face at the window, the length of time Mr. Nadow was holding her hand between his two large ones, holding her gaze with his sharp, blue eyes. She could not speak. All her words were trapped in her throat.

It took at least a day for her to be able to speak normally, not to stutter or hesitate between phrases. And no matter how friendly or encouraging he was, Emma remained a little in awe of Jack Nadow. "What should we try today?" he would say in his New York drawl when he arrived mid-morning. "What do you think? A zinc plate?" He was a short man with a disproportionately thick neck and muscular arms which he'd wave when he made a point. "I want them like my paintings – expanses." Emma etched four lines along each edge like a rough border, a scrawl on one side. Sprays of transparent ink, layer printed over layer: violet, then dark green, then white, then lavender, precise technical work that produced – magic. The first proof came off the press and was hung on the rack to dry.

What next? he'd say. What colours, what order, what do you think?

How about a broad streak of light through the middle this time? she ventured. How about blue, ochre, then purple? And again, at the end of the process, when they held the sheet in their hands, they had magical colour, rhythmically pulsing, radiant, shimmering colour.

Emma was wild with happiness. Each morning, as she rode to the studio on her bicycle through the green streets of the town, she imagined herself a heroine setting out on an adventure, a quest that would test her mettle. Her legs peddled furiously. She flew from the studio to the gourmet deli to pick up a tasty lunch for the two of them. The summer days were hot and humid, yet she ran to the art department storeroom to search for another shade, another texture of off-white paper. And, she ran back, her arms full.

How about a stripe on that side? How about blue, green, brown, yellow then red? Sometimes it didn't work, sometimes the print came out spotty, opaque, leaden, but always Jack listened, consulted.

Emma wanted to tell everyone, anyone: I'm collaborating with this man with the greying hair and the pointy beard, this famous man, I'm holding my own, ME.

Her parents were away on a summer-long car trip, visiting a cousin in Chicago, an aunt in Texas, crossing America. She imagined their Chrysler barreling down narrow roads bisecting fields of tall wheat, her mother'd be driving, sunglasses and cigarette in place, her father would be reading aloud from a guidebook: my, we're approaching a historic burg, Deerlope. That was his most constant tone, sardonic amusement. His elfin face fell naturally into a cheerful expression, but it was cheer at the foolishness and pretensions of his fellow man. She tended to be mournful in her disdain: the last motel had mould growing between the tiles, yesterday's lunch was so greasy her stomach still hurt.

With her parents lost to the open road and most of her friends scattered for the summer, Emma had to resort to long distance. She phoned her current best friend, Courtney, in New York, thinking as she dialed that for once she had something that could match one of her friend's stories. But as Emma started babbling about the wonderful, brilliant Mr. Nadow, Courtney cut in with "all that colour field stuff is outdated. Don't you know, it's not where it's at?"

"What do you mean?" Emma was honestly mystified. What did fashion have to do with it?

"That narrowness. It's been exploded. Photorealism, op, pop – "

"Vulgarity."

"Irreverent, whimsical. . . ."

"Trite," Emma insisted.

"Listen to me, oh-straight-one, I know. I've been going to the galleries. I'm everywhere; yesterday, I was at the Factory." Courtney had met Warhol, pasty faced, wigged Warhol. She hadn't spoken to him, but she had attended this fantastic party crammed with fantastic people: models, rock 'n' roll singers, designers. She'd watched someone take raunchy pictures of two nude, stoned girls; she'd danced, DANCED a few feet from Jim Morrison; she'd caught a glimpse of a young man shooting up. "What a scene," she said. "I'm thinking of dropping acid. Why don't you come to New York? We could do it together. Expand our consciousness."

Emma thought of the prints she was making with Jack and the way the colours they created seemed to expand and expand until they threatened to slip over the paper edge and sail off into infinity. She needed to talk, not to party.

After a sequence of phone calls, she found Velga in Yonkers. "You haven't come for a visit in ages," said Emma.

"Well, I'm dying to see you too," said Velga, who had turned back into Velga and cast off the name Marianne only two years ago. "But I'm doing summer stock, glory be, all summer."

Their lives had developed in different directions since

Brooklyn. Velga had grown into a long, lean, Nordic beauty and was encouraged to depend on that, rather than her brains, for her future. Her parents hadn't left Brooklyn, and Velga, as a member of both a Latvian folk dance group and a choir, was a frequent attender of Latvian songfests. At the first beauty pageant she entered, Miss Teen New York City, she sang the mournful *Set Early Sun* for the talent portion. She was not chosen as a finalist, even though (if she said so herself) she filled her swimsuit better than any of the others. The next pageant, New York Junior Miss, she chose to sing a medley from *Hair* and won. Next she was a semi-finalist for Miss New York State and might have gone further if she had answered the question "If you had the chance to meet President Johnson, what would you tell him?" with something bland about peace and harmony rather than speaking about the importance of the U.S. retaining their policy of non-recognition of the Soviet incorporation of the Baltic states. Stung, Velga gave up on beauty pageants and forged on to car and boat shows, regional commercials, and acting lessons.

"He's very important," Emma told Velga. "He's a major artist."

"I know what you mean," her friend said. "There's this director I'm working on. . . ."

"No," Emma said. "Not like that, no."

She and Jack were collaborators in the production of art. Even if separated by age and talent, they spoke as equals, arguing the how and why. He valued her opinions, and she loved to hear his stories of other artists.

He told of Pollock's pissing into Peggy Guggenheim's fireplace. He joked about Newman and Rothko's spiritual pretensions. He made rude comments about a certain pretty abstract painter and a prominent critic. He invited Emma for dinner at the apartment where he was staying.

She watched him cook: spaghetti and salad and garlic toast. She sipped her wine, as he downed his, and she listened, excited by the familiarity and authority his easy judgements implied.

They sat on the floor to eat, facing each other across the coffee table. Jack did not gaze into her eyes. The conversation remained slightly malicious but impersonal. She was unaware that her attentiveness, her questions, the strength of her laugh were being wilfully misread. Then, as he was serving her a dish of ice cream, he dropped down beside her. He grabbed her by the shoulders and pulled her in. His actions were so sudden and so disconnected from everything that had gone on before between them that she was disoriented, confused. It was only after he had been kissing her for a moment or two that her head cleared enough to realize she didn't want this. She tried to pull away. He held on, his lips on her throat, one hand tight on her arm, the other already under her skirt, fingers frantically busy.

"You're hurting me," she said. "Please," she said. She started to struggle, to use her strength. One big shove and he fell back. She jumped up and looked down at him sprawled on the carpet, his zipper open, his cock shrivelling.

She turned and ran out the door, down the hall. She could hear him coming after her, wheezing a little. "I didn't mean . . . Emma, this is silly. Emma!" She was at the front door. She fumbled with her bike lock. For a second, she could not remember the combination. "Emma, I don't understand."

She lifted her head and looked at him. "Don't worry," she said. "Everything's cool," she said. "I'll see you tomorrow." And she was on her bike and off, wobbling a little, down the street.

Was she unusually obtuse? She had been so surprised. And he, she smiled remembering his expression when she shoved him off, had been even more surprised by her lack of interest. He never hid that he was married or that he was dedicated to his three children. Yet he expected gratitude, compliance. That must be what he was used to: getting his way.

At the time, riding home through the dark streets wet with rain, lying awake listening to the sounds of the empty house, she thought she'd acted the only way she could. Her response had been not moral but instinctive. By the next day she was beginning to see it would have been smarter to think, to calculate, before she reacted.

Jack arrived later than usual. "How did you sleep?" he asked, his eyes a clear and innocent blue. "Fine," her answer was weak, automatic, a lie. She went back to grinding the surface of a lithostone. He checked over yesterday's proofs. There was none of the usual chat, nor did he ask her opinion.

When she finished the rinse, she stood and waited. He was still staring at the lithographs. "Jack." She could hear her heartbeat.

He hesitated ever so slightly before answering. "Yes?"

"What would you like to try today?"

He glanced over at the clock. "Give me a minute."

The far door swung open. The print professor strode in followed by a darkhaired shadow – Cheryl Klein, Emma's constant competition for top marks in the art program. Cheryl was tiny, intense, an essence, as if everything superfluous had boiled away. Like canned soup, Emma once complained to Courtney; you need to add something to make her palatable. Cheryl was there to help, to make things more efficient, Jack said in explanation to Emma. "We'll explore, the three of us."

Sure we will, Emma thought. And she spent the last few days of Jack's residency watching him lean over Cheryl as she worked, his hand casually on her shoulder, or if Emma turned away and busied herself with a task, listening to their voices intertwine. "Not a bad idea," Jack said to Cheryl, "Let's try it but. . . ."

So many years later, it was those lithographs, those beautiful, radiant lithographs that she had made for and with Jack Nadow that she found in the catalogue. All the other prints in the book carried acknowledgements: printed by so and so, published by such and such, but not hers.

A couple of days later, in an art magazine her mother had also brought, Emma read an interview with the now famous Cheryl Klein. Cheryl spoke of how she began in the art world by doing colour field painting but changed mediums once her conciousness was raised. Now, she defined herself as a third-generation feminist, who having the mental freedom the older generations did not, was not interested in traditional female work: "repetition, domesticity, boredom, that's in the past." For you, Emma thought, irritated at Cheryl's cavalier insistence that things had changed so much for women. At the same time, she felt a queasy envy of what her old classmate had achieved. Emma felt she'd had a chance and hadn't taken it, while Cheryl Klein, who'd been less fastidious, was representing the U.S. at international art shows.

Still, Emma knew it was (always) more complicated. She remembered the dazzled expression on Cheryl's face when she gazed up at Jack Nadow. Her response to the artist had seemed honest: her attraction to him looked real. And why not? A mentor, a master, a lord of the coveted kingdom. The mystery was why Emma had felt admiration and respect but not *it*, not that sexual current. Had she not dreamt of a man who would be her teacher and guide? Someone older, wiser. Of course, when Mr. Knightly declared himself to Emma Woodhouse, he did not pounce: he spoke in a tone of "sincere tenderness." Nor did he have a wife and three children; not that Emma had thought of Jack's dependents when she pushed him away.

Frankie, Juris, the two or three other men she responded to: each one of them was a surprise and not at all what she thought she wanted.

The heart has its reasons

Cheryl Klein had shaped black rubber tubing into letters that spelled the saying across a slashed, white plastic sheet. It was with such "installations," as she called them, words written in unexpected media: rags, tacks, styrofoam, dried twigs, that she became a commercial and artistic success. The words always formed statements: slogans, instant wisdom, digest versions of Western and Eastern thought. One series, etched on bronze plaques or carved into slabs of stone, consisted of one-line summaries of fifty Great Books. Now, the magazine said, she was taking her art out of the galleries and bringing it to the masses with electronic signboards at airports, hotels, the Spectacolor board of Times Square. The words formed and dissolved, on and

off
DON'T LIVE ON CREDIT
on and
off
SAVE ME FROM WHAT I WANT
on   five seconds
off
BEWARE OF PLEASURE

CHOOSE YOUR THRILLS CAREFULLY
off
THERE'S NO SUCH THING AS FAIR PLAY

III

In the thirteenth century, the Germans, with the Pope's support, organized a holy crusade against the Latvians. Christianity and foreign rule were forced upon them. But a fondness for the old pagan religion survived (and even today in Soviet Latvia and through the rest of the world, *Dievturi* – followers – practice the old faith). The foundation of this faith was a moral one, one's "disposition towards self, others and the world." This foundation, the sacred codes of conduct, was not handed down by a supreme god, not "revealed," but transmitted by one's ancestors and learned through life. The ancient Latvians did, however, worship three divine beings: *Dievs*, God of the heavens; *Mara*, Goddess of the earth; and *Laime/a*, Goddess of Fate, as well as a few minor deities such as *Saule*, the Sun.

Mrs. Avendemis's visit was more of a help than Emma would admit. With her mother at home, she felt freer, less tied to the house. She could go to an exercise class and not have to rush, skipping a shower because she had to pick up Michael, cutting off a conversation because Harry was due home from school. Her life was such, shapeless and over-regimented, too full and too empty, that she felt relief at even such a relative loosening of responsibilities.

Spring had finally arrived. Everything was brown and ugly, the trees still leafless, the roads strewn with dust and debris. Tap water carried the taste of winter garbage rotting in the river. But at least the snow was gone; the air was gentle, almost mild. Emma drove out to the shops. To the genteel antique and handicraft boutiques of 124th, to the funkier local designer outlets, health food and bookstores of Whyte Avenue.

If she was feeling particularly anxious, she drove to West Edmonton Mall, the Great Land of Kitsch, gobbler of time and taste: midway rides, dolphins, submarines, crown jewels, a European and a New Orleans street, a Spanish galleon, and a tropical beach. The fake and the falsified she thought, though not on the days when she'd been reading the latest art magazines. Then she saw the mall as the one place in Edmonton that expressed the postmodern spirit of the age, a representation of representations, an imitation of imitations. Everything once, twice, three times removed from the real. *(What's that?)* The authentic. *(Does it exist?)* Chain and department stores, knock down furniture and tacked together clothes, copies of copies, cookies, yogurt, tropical fish, exotic birds, eat with your greasy fingers burgers, dogs, fast, fake, and jumbled; buy, consume, simulacrum of simulacra of life, experience, food, shrunk to a T-shirt.

When the going gets tough, the tough go
shopping.
Die, Yuppie scum.
Reeboks, because life is not a spectator sport.
Bloomingdale's or bust
Kiss me, I'm Italian
Born to shop

She walked down the imitation boulevards until her
edginess was blunted, exhausted by the brightness of the
lights, the din of the fountains, the sheer distance:
megamall, megakitsch, mega blank out.

But her favourite shops were the ritzy stores of
downtown: cream coloured and hushed, with lots of dark
wood and French scent in the air. This is no cheap thrill,
these shops said; this is serious. Blu's, Avorio, Holt
Renfrew, Henry Singer. High fashion ready to wear – like a
magical wand, ready to transform the nondescript into the
elegant, the uncertain into the confident, the plain into the
beautiful or, at least, the less plain.

Emma bought a set of dishes, white with a delicate
blue line, an arrangement of dried pink roses and
delphiniums, black and white minimalist patterned sheets
for their bed. She bought a couple of Italian shirts for Juris;
she bought new jeans and a video game for the boys. She
bought a dove grey silk-chiffon blouse, a black lace
nightgown, a trench coat, four Calvin Klein briefs and two
bras, and a clutch of handcrafted earrings, including one
that was an imitation of a Greek *caryatid* that hung to her
shoulders and a pair that consisted of a miniature Mona
Lisa for one ear and an artist's palette for the other. "A
woman," she told Laila, "can never have too many
earrings."

"Aren't these a bit youthful for you? Almost gaudy," her
mother said.

Emma laughed and held a particularly glittery pair up to her ears. She confessed that what she really wanted, what she craved, were simple diamond studs, big enough to be noticed, but not so big as to be vulgar, a carat or two each would be nice. But you couldn't buy yourself diamond earrings. They should be a gift. They should have a symbolic meaning.

And thinking of such meanings, her mood changed. She no longer felt soothed, appeased, but surfeited. Her stomach ached. Her skin was clammy. All her tasteful purchases, as she put them away, looked reduced, inadequate. She began to add up how much she had charged, but just making the list made her so jumpy that she tore up all the charge slips without ever coming to a final addition. She vowed to put away her cards and use only cash; she vowed to stop. They had everything they needed, everything. No more *stuff*, no more.

INTERRUPTION

What was Madame Bovary guilty of? Why did Flaubert need to punish his creation so thoroughly, so horribly? Compare the quick, almost merciful end that Tolstoy gave his Anna to the days of agony Flaubert put Emma through. He's a sadist, I thought the first time I read *Madame Bovary*, and I still find the section almost too painful to read.

Is it because Emma commits adultery, that offense against family and bourgeois society? The novel as a moral, cautionary tale: that reading is a popular one, popular and superficial. Flaubert was not Tolstoy; he did not believe in chastity or the good of the community. He was an enthusiastic visitor of brothels; when with the Egyptian whore Kuchiouk, it was the vermin on her body that he found the "most bewitching touch of all." "Adultery," he told the married Louise Colet, "is glorious, it is revolt against the most bourgeois and detestable of institutions." He was speaking in mid-seduction yet, even allowing for the necessities of the moment; I believe that Flaubert was sincere when he spoke of the word *adultery* as "fragrant with a peculiar magic, full of a supreme poetry compounded of voluptuousness and blasphemy." It was ambiguity, violation that he was drawn to.

This impulse, an old and familiar one which links sexuality and degradation, does not, of course, preclude Flaubert's condemning Emma for her infidelity. In fact, it is this impulse which makes men divide women into the respectable and the sensual, the mother and the whore. Flaubert was, after all, a man of his century; he kept his mother and his mistress resolutely apart no matter how much Colet begged to be introduced to Madame Flaubert.

Still, whether he was a believer in the double standard or not, in his letters he says (or, at least, he gives the excuse) that he lost respect for Louise not because of her sexuality or her previous or present lovers; no, it was her lack of literary taste, her stupid comments which infuriated him.

Again, for Flaubert, stupidity was the mortal sin. Emma Bovary is condemned for her illusions. She takes from the romantic novels form and content for her amorphous longing. As she is dying, she complains repeatedly of the taste of ink, and after her death, a flood of black liquid streams from her mouth. What are we to make of this? Has Flaubert suddenly become a writer of the twentieth century rather than the nineteenth, reminding us that Emma is a creation of his pen, left lifeless and disfigured by a trail of ink? Or is it more symbolic? Has she imbibed so deeply of these books that they have poisoned her?

Flaubert was one of a long line of men warning women against the insidious effect of romances, a line that stretches through Samuel Johnson, who in the *Rambler* created Imperia, a proud woman ruined by reading romances, to today's husband who sneers at his wife's viewing of "Knots Landing." Yet, like Johnson who blamed his own unsettled state of mind on the romances he liked to read, Flaubert himself was a devoted reader of romantic novels. And his great novel, which – as he said – taught a clear lesson and certainly deplored the effect of romantic books, was in itself considered too deplorable for a ladv to read.

No one ever seems to worry about men reading a particular work. I suppose they are considered strong enough not to be tempted, formed enough not to have ideas put into their heads. No, probably the point is that it doesn't matter if ideas are put into a man's head. There is no danger in that. I heard a man once say of his wife, "If I hadn't let her go to university . . ." implying that if he had prevented her, she would never have left him. If she hadn't read/studied/thought. . . . But the book (the studying, the friend) does not give rise to the longing. The longing is first, soil and seed.

Flaubert shared more with his heroine than a taste for certain books. He longed for a heightened existence. In his way, he desired escape from dreary daily life; he desired transcendence, as much as Emma did. In his youth, he wrote of longing to be a woman or an ancient Greek, an emperor or sultan, "with absolute power over a thousand slaves." During the time he was forced to attend law school, he was struck down with episodes called "fits" by his doctors. These episodes always followed the same pattern: first, a golden light, then, terror at what felt like "the ebbing away of his personality and the approach of annihilation." He would fall unconscious for hours and would awaken to weakness and depression. The depressions would last for weeks and were probably intensified by the contrast between what he experienced during the time he'd been unable to move or speak, an explosion of images and thoughts – golden dreams, he called them, "a combination of Saint Theresa, Hoffman and Edgar Poe," and what he awoke to, the grey monotony of his daily life. At least the fits released him, by making him seem unfit, from the exigencies of a profession or a social life. His father gave him permission to dedicate his life to writing, and he had no more attacks.

Emma Bovary is condemned for her illusion that she can be fulfilled in the here and now. She is guilty of desiring passion, perfect passion. When being a dutiful wife, a fond mother does not fill the emptiness inside, she casts aside these roles to play another female stereotype – slave of love. Flaubert sought completion for his emptiness in a more male fashion: in his work. He'd spend a day worrying over a sentence, a week sweating over a paragraph (while she tastes ink as she dies, he, writing the death scene with pen and ink, wrote "with a strong taste of arsenic in my mouth"). He wanted language "to move the stars to pity," but found it "a cracked kettle on which we beat our tunes." He desired perfection, but it eluded him as it eluded Emma.

When Flaubert was asked once too often on whom Emma Bovary was based, he answered crabbily, *Madame Bovary, c'est moi.* And he spoke more truly than perhaps even he knew. In the detached, factual way he described her death, he punished her and he punished himself.

Then, a week later, on her way to Safeway, she heard an ad for a Mother's Day sale. Mother's Day and her mother leaving so soon. Emma was overwhelmed with sentiment. She drove past the supermarket, up 109th, down the hill and across the river not to the sale but to the little galleries of downtown. She bought her mother an art nouveau, silver snuff box to use for her pills. She bought her father (she'd missed his birthday) a 2,000-year-old terracotta oil lamp, wishing him always, she wrote, the light of understanding and signing herself a once foolish maiden.

After her mother went home, Emma bought two large paintings both by local women artists. One was an opulent nude, a play in rich, sensual colour, peaches and pinks and golds, delivered in agitated, lively brushstrokes. The other was a precise portrait of a ghoulish looking woman in chalky, acid tinged tones, under an ink grey sky.

"Yin and yang." Emma said. "Body and mind."

"They're too big," Juris said. "Too domineering."

"They're not. They're just right. It's our house that's too small. Cramped. I feel cramped all the time. It's O.K. for you at the lab day and night. We need more room. I'm serious. Why don't we visit some show homes?"

"Will you calm down, please. We're not buying a new house. We can't afford a new house. Besides you know I need to be close to work."

"This shack's falling to bits. Tiles coming up in the bathroom. Cupboard doors that won't close properly. The front steps are collapsing. I can't stand it. I can't. Where are you going? We're talking. You can't just go."

"You should hear yourself. Your voice has gone all high pitched and shrill. Shrewish."

"Damn you. I can't help my voice. I'm a woman. It gets high pitched when I'm upset. You're just trying to avoid the issue."

"There's no issue. We aren't looking at houses. We're in debt as it is. You have to control yourself. We're reaching the limit on all of our cards. It's as clear as day. There's no choice."

In traditional Latvian society, men and women were equal, separate but equal. Was this unusual egalitarianism fostered by the ancient Latvian worship of *Mara*, Mother Earth? (For her worship predated that of the other two main deities.) Did Mother Goddess worship lead to a deeply ingrained cultural respect for women? Or did the cultural respect lead to the worship? Which came first? In Graeco-Roman mythology, the all important Sun was male, while the inconstant moon was female. In contrast, in Latvian mythology, the Sun is female and the moon male. Moreover, the Sun is often addressed in a familiar, affectionate way: *Saulite*, the diminutive of *Saule*, as if you were speaking to a favourite aunt or a precious older sister.

The argument was becoming habitual: Emma pleading for some essential item, Juris recalling their recent expenses, the Saab had needed a valve job, the refrigerator had had to be replaced. Now and then, if Emma was in mid-guilt attack, she would be the one insisting they must control their spending and he arguing for a new, efficient car/dishwasher/camera. Both veered between extravagance and parsimony, indifference and panic. Juris did not care about things; he would wear the same shirt and jeans for months if given the chance. He would mould himself to a sagging armchair rather than buy a new one. But he was chronically preoccupied with his research and did not or could not put his mind to budgets or discount stores or details like booking air tickets far enough ahead to get the cheap flights. If he needed something, it should be instantly available to him. Avoiding hassles was worth money, was worth anything, to him. So Juris never concerned himself with finances except for his monthly attempt to pay the bills. Then he panicked.

Meanwhile, Emma's spend and regret cycle had a more personal and compulsive rhythm. She wanted to be able to control herself and all her impulses. But why did she always have to deprive herself, when she felt so deprived already?

At the end of their finances fight the month before, just after Juris shot out the front door and drove off to his lab, Laila had put her hand on her daughter's shoulder and said, "How about some camomile tea?" And when they were sitting mugs in hand, Laila pulled a check out of her skirt pocket.

"Mother, I can't. It's not right."

"Don't worry; there's a catch. I want Andrejs – for the summer."

"He's still – "

"If you insist on raising, or not raising your children, letting them wallow in a barbarous state, I must insist on my time with them. My time and a little time at camp."

"God, that place still exists? Hiking and singing Latvian songs in the Catskills?"

"He'll come back with some manners and more Latvian. You'll see."

"Come on. They're not so bad."

"They are."

"So you're going to rent them, one by one?"

"Rent and renovate."

"I bet you can't."

"As a child, you had wonderful manners. We could take you anywhere. And your Latvian! Other parents would congratulate us."

"We shouldn't have moved from Brooklyn if that was all you wanted: Latvian America. But, as I recall, that narrow little community was starting to get to you."

Twice Laila opened her mouth and seemed about to speak. Finally she said, "Everything gets to me at one time or another."

"You and me both." And mother and daughter shared a rueful smile.

"We wanted so much for you," Laila said. "And that involved the limitless American horizon, not tribal boundaries. Or that's what we thought – then."

"And look at me." Emma passed a hand gracefully over her face. "Exiled in a different way."

"Don't you compare the two. They're not comparable, my experience and yours."

"Fine. You tried hard, both you and Dad. I'll never say you didn't."

That seemed to remind Laila of another source of resentment. "What about all your amber? You want jewellery; you talk to me about earrings. What about the amber we've given you? Our relatives, our friends. Beautiful. Unmatchable. I never see you wear it. Have you sold it? Given it away?"

"Come on, Mum. It's not me."

"The tears of the Daughters of the Sun."

"I have my hoard. Do you want to see? I do take it out. Sometimes when I'm very upset. I put a brooch in my pocket. Sort of a talisman."

"But you don't wear it."

"It's too ethnic."

"I don't know what you're talking about."

"I've seen too many old women wearing cheap flowered dresses and amber necklaces. I can't." Then, seeing her mother's face. "Not you. I didn't mean you. In malls, I see them wandering about the malls."

To make amends, Emma took the check. Besides, she reasoned, they had left that argument so far behind that to not accept it would seem even more ungrateful. Emma put it away. Several times, in an offhand voice, she thanked her mother. As soon as Laila was on the plane, Emma used the money not to pay off bills but to buy the paintings.

Amber has always been precious to the Latvians. From neolithic times, they have gathered the fossil resin from the Baltic shore and used it for ornamentation and trade and medicinal purposes. Perhaps because amber is golden and warm to the touch, it has always been associated with the gentle Sun. *Saulite.*

Now there is no folk culture . . .

"These are gifts," she told Juris. "For the spirit. Necessary and beautiful. Be thankful I haven't been bit by the renovation bug. Now that can ruin a family," she told Juris.

For it did seem that every house on the block was being stripped down to its black plastic and wire shell. The sound of power drills and crashing plaster filled the spring air. Janie and her family were sleeping in the basement as everything on the two upper floors was being ripped apart and reassembled. Frances was having another floor added. Still, making sure everyone understood that she was the sensible, shrewd woman she'd always been, she told everyone that she'd found a dirt-cheap company, that'd given them an incredibly low bid. (Only $45,000.) Janie and Frances who never spoke to each other were overheard discussing ceramic tile outlets. Maria, whose husband had insisted they wait another year, wandered the neighbourhood with a tape measure, actually measuring the lengths of the extensions. "Ours will be better. We are talking to an architect. Ours will be bigger. Very expensive."

only ersatz, only kitsch

Making a point to Juris about her willingness to be fiscally prudent, Emma gave up her aerobics class. Actually, she had been ready to quit. What had charmed her when she started, the perkiness, the electronic music, the optimistic "we-can-do-it" atmosphere, now bored and irritated her.

She took up walking. She put on her sneakers and her Walkman and strode off through the neighbourhood to the strains of rhythm and blues. She usually headed for Saskatchewan Drive, where she could walk along the cusp of the hill and look out over the valley or follow a narrow dirt path through brush and woods down to the river. If she turned off the Walkman, she could hear the traffic on the freeways that lined and crossed the valley. Otherwise once in the trees she was in the country, sharp green, scented, and a relief from the (sensual) deprivation of the long Edmonton winter.

Hold me, touch me, she hummed along with her tape. *Love me, now.* She had dozens of these tapes (Whitney Houston, Otis Redding, Percy Sledge, Natalie Cole, Luther Van Drossen, Peaches and Herb, Roberta Flack, Peabo Bryson), all the plaintive black singers, pop singers, whose voices caressed, coloured the sentimental lyrics with centuries of yearning. Juris hated her new tapes, though he enjoyed Chicago and Delta Blues and gospel: authentic, traditional music, Folkways records, not commercial sludge. Real art, he'd say, not kitsch, borrowing one of her terms. They're too loud and hysterical, he'd complain. And she did like to play them at full volume, so the string-boosted melodies would sweep her up, carry her off. Float-along-with-me tunes. Her feet hit the grass in rhythm, *I want to feel/I want to dance/I want to move/With you.* And she did, she did, she did want to dance – away.

Hold me, touch me	A woman's voice
Love me, now.	rippling with longing
No time to waste	A strong, seductive male voice
No joy to lose	
I'll love you	
Now	the voices interweaving
Fill me with ecstasy	intertwining
Show me the rapture	blending
No time to waste	
No joy to lose	
Tonight	

Now, they sang, now: gratification, completion. This moment. She could feel the words along the paths of her nerves. *Hold me.* Her arms and legs ached with yearning. *Touch me.*

A square-jawed, square-shouldered jogger smiled at her as he ran past. As if he could tell what she'd been thinking. Maybe, she'd been smiling – or simpering, that was probably it. Her expression had been so foolish that he'd been moved to grin. She had seen him before a couple of times, loping along, but then he'd never given her a glance. She rewound her tape. Once more, *Fill me.* . . . She never grew tired of this song, *with ecstasy.* . . .

She wondered who he was, for he did look as if he were someone, not just another earnest and friendly Belgravean. A solidly built, light-eyed, stubborn-mouthed someone.

Emma was suddenly conscious of more than her facial expression. She must look like a bright and bulbous jelly bean in the green sweatsuit. And with the wind, her hair was probably a mess.

The next day, and from then on, she applied makeup before she went on her walk. She bound her hair back with a silk holder, and since her long legs were still one of her best features, she wore shorts even when it was cool and rainy. For a week there was no sign of him. Emma tried earlier, then later, but still no jogger. Finally, one bright evening, she was in her cool-down, ambling more than walking, when he passed her. He looked back. He didn't smile, but he took her in, head to toe. Then he was off.

Emma speeded up. He was much faster, even when she gave it her all. She was soon sweaty and breathless. But she kept her eye on his receding back, and she followed. He crossed Whyte; he crossed 87th to a part of the drive that she rarely reached. She was gasping noisily. He was way ahead, a tiny figure, when finally he crossed the road, sprinted up a long driveway and disappeared.

She stopped two houses away and stared. It was huge and new, an imitation Victorian with light blue vinyl siding and a brighter blue door. Its long, narrow windows glinted in the sunset; the entire house seemed to glow with pink and gold light, a pastel confection that quoted so obliquely the mansions she had passed, and wondered about as a girl.

Let us gather flags, more flags, more flags than we are.

Tears of the Daughters of the Sun. *Saulite.*

Though the term was over, Juris was busier than ever. Besides attending a rash of administrative meetings, he was spending longer and longer hours in the lab. He had decided several years before to search for the genetic trigger for diabetes, that is, the various genes that when combined cause the disease. His lab was using as subjects a group of interrelated Mennonite families with a high incidence of juvenile diabetes, who lived in an isolated town close to the border of the Northwest Territories. The group was a find; they had intermarried for generations and rarely had an outsider added to the genetic mix.

The first steps, begun three years before, had involved producing a gigantic family tree that went back to the 1600s. All known cases of autoimmune disease were marked. Juris, his postdoctoral fellow, and his graduate student flew into the town several times, first to interview, then to take blood. Back at the lab, the white cells, the lymphocytes, were extracted from the blood. Then the postdoc transformed the cells, by way of a virus, into growing and multiplying cell lines. For two years these lines were tested against a genetic marker (composed of DNA fragments that worked as probes). Finally, Juris could announce that all the relatives with diabetes had the same DQ 3,2ß genetic sequence. But the inquiry was just beginning. Not everyone with this gene variation had diabetes. Other unknowns were contributing.

Juris was convinced that there was another gene, or a set of genes, that controlled susceptibility to autoimmune reactions. This gene, he thought, predisposed the immune system to react to what should remain unnoticed, and then the DQ 3,2ß gene predetermined that it attacked the pancreas to create diabetes. There were no probes for this gene. It was all his hypothesis. But he felt he was right; he felt it was possible for him to make this great discovery. In a few months of testing the class of white blood cells known as T-cells (they actually attack foreign entities) Juris and his lab found that all his subjects with diabetes had a certain receptor. There were many genes in the T-cell. One of them close to the receptor site could be the one he was searching for. But to find it, this trigger to so much physical suffering, he needed a broader range of subjects and the means for an intensive search: more assistants, more lab space, more funding just when the university and the federal funding agencies were administering massive cutbacks.

Juris was going to various conferences (traveling the world, while I'm stuck at home was how Emma saw it) delivering papers on his findings on the DQ 3,2ß sequence, drawing respectful attention. It was pleasant but not enough. Though he did not delve into his hypothesis about the "autoimmune" gene, others, he was sure, would soon be searching (probably already were) in the same area. And with his funding problems, they would be able to overtake him. The breakthrough, with its potential to break him through to a level and a position he had always wanted, would belong to someone else.

Received Ideas, Edmonton – Science 1988
Science is more demanding than any mistress could be.
Science demands total dedication and punishes any lack of diligence.
Scientists don't cheat.
Bend the observation to fit the theory.
Publish or perish.

In graduate school, even earlier, Juris had been sure that his career would be if not brilliant, at least significant. He stood out as a student, easily winning prizes and scholarships, and he'd expected, without thinking much about it and certainly without planning, that his prominence would continue. Looking back, his certainty seemed not so much arrogant as naive. In the past, the best students, after their Ph.D. and a couple of years of postdocs, had wonderful positions offered to them; they often didn't even have to apply. By the time he graduated, the times and the number of positions available had changed. After three years of waiting, three years of working as a postdoc in someone else's lab, Juris found himself not at Stanford or Johns Hopkins but at the University of Alberta, "which ain't so bad," as he needlessly told Emma, "but it ain't top drawer either."

His father was disappointed. "I presumed. . . ," he said when told of the move. "I thought. . . ." He did not have to explain further. His expectations of Juris had always been clear and enormous. He closed his eyes for a moment. He lifted one shoulder in a defensive tic. Juris had seen both gestures countless times. When his father rose to leave the room, the leg with the shrapnel dragged even more than usual. "The facilities are wonderful," Juris called after him. His father's face expressed only exhaustion.

Too many generations lay between Juris and his father. Andrejs Zeps was an old man. The wounded leg came from the first, not the second world war. He'd been raised in a nineteenth century household, raised to duty and seriousness. The family was upper middle class, intellectual and deeply involved in the struggle for Latvian determination, for freedom from the German barons and the Russian czar. His uncle spent his life producing the first Latvian dictionary. His father was the publisher of a nationalistic newspaper. From childhood on, Andrejs Zeps was told he was going to be a doctor. The Latvian people needed doctors; tuberculosis was a constant scourge. Perhaps Andrejins (little Andrejs), he remembered his grandmother saying, stroking his head, will be the one to find the solution.

He never considered *not* becoming a doctor. Botany was his true passion, cultivated on long summer holidays at the family's country home, but botany could be no more than a hobby, expressed only in his preference for herbal remedies. In comparison to later deprivations, this one was minor. For, like so many others, his life after 1939 became an exploration of the discipline of loss. He grew to discriminate between gradations, degrees, variations: he lost his professorship of medicine, his home, his freedom; he lost relatives, friends, culture, and while he was imprisoned, he lost his five-year-old daughter.

He escaped with his pregnant wife to Germany and the refugee camps, where he worked night and day as a doctor. He was lucky, he knew, that he retained, like a kernel at the centre of a peeled onion, mind and health, Maya and Juris. Though Maya was not the girl he married that could lighten his seriousness with her laughter. After years of being tossed about, driftwood on the sea of history, she'd grown querulous and afraid.

And Andrejs, himself, once he arrived in America, felt that instead of sailing into safe harbour, he'd washed up on an alien shore. He had little English and no chance of practising his profession. He was in his mid-fifties: too old, too late, washed up.

Juris knew all this of his father. As an adult he knew it. As a child he felt it. He could not remember the details of the series of apartments they lived in, where or what he played, anything of his early school years. So much was gone. But certain scenes, a few lit moments in the expanse of unhappy grey, were always with him. His father at the supper table, eating methodically. His mother wiping the washed dishes, the doorknobs, the covers of his schoolbooks with rubbing alcohol. "Maya, sit," His father said. "Your dinner's getting cold."

"Let me finish," his mother said. "I have to finish. I have to stop the germs. They infiltrate, and then they attack."

"You're getting worse. How can I eat in this stink? Maya . . ." He slammed his fist down on the table. "Sit."

She sat. "I'm being careful."

"I work all day for what? At least, we can have a proper dinner when I get home."

"I can't eat." Her fork in mid air. "My stomach is worse and worse. . . ."

"It is not," his father said, "that I am ashamed of working on the line." (For he worked in a factory, drilling together mechanical horses for supermarkets and shopping centres.) "All freely chosen work has its dignity. But it's the uselessness, the waste."

Juris could not look at his mother's face. He stared at his plate. His throat was closed, and the stew meat was heavy and thick and unswallowable in his mouth. He jumped up and ran off to the bathroom to spit and flush.

"What did I tell you?" his mother said. "You see how pale he is? He's caught a bug. You see?"

Anxiety, that was what he remembered, both at home and at school where he was teased for his accent and his odd clothes. Anxiety and the prickling smell of rubbing alcohol.

Gradually their situation improved. His father took an exam and became a lab technician. His mother began to give piano lessons. They stayed in one apartment long enough for Juris to begin to make friends. After all, he was learning how to move his mouth and tongue like the others, learning to sound and look American. Still, his father, more than ever, preached the doctrine of accomplishment. Juris was to do the great things Andrejs had been prevented from doing. And his mother, she remained convinced that outside the family, all was threatening and dangerous. She was permanently on guard at the door of their apartment, disinfectant in hand.

By the time Juris was in high school, his father had begun to work on an encyclopedia of the plants of Latvia. Andrejs worked late into the night in the corner of his bedroom on a small table that overflowed with paper and index cards. Through memory and library books, disconnected from other botanists or even an academic education in the subject, Andrejs was trying to piece together a master work, the first study of the flora and fauna of the countryside he would never see again. He worked for years doggedly, grimly, almost desperately. He was locked, he was sure, in battle with the forces that intended to obliterate Latvia from the face of the earth. As if his documenting, his recording of the specific and the actual, could preserve the abstract and the indefinable. And as the years passed and Andrejs seemed no closer to getting a publisher or even completing his work, Juris began to feel that his father was not doing scientific work but, like a Borgean character, a solitary man in a dynasty of solitary men, documenting the botany of a place that didn't exist, his own *Tlon*, making the imaginary real through his will.

Typically, Juris did not keep his vision to himself. He began to rib his father about his "great fantasy" until Andrejs admitted he was unhappy that his book was arising not from concrete observation, that basis of scientific endeavour, but from ever more distant memories. He felt the need, he said, to get out, observe, note, describe; he felt the need to do things in the proper way, and, as if taking up Juris' challenge, he set himself another task. With his leg, he couldn't walk into forest or make his way through underbrush. He had to have easy access. So it was for practical reasons that he chose to study adventive plants along railroad rights of way.

Adventive plants are immigrant plants, *introduced accidently, not native, imperfectly naturalized (as in being unable to bear fully mature fruit)*. Andrejs studied how seeds were carried from one region to another. He observed where, how and on what ground they fell. He took samples for more minute observation. He returned to record whether they took root, reproduced, became – over the years – indigenous. It's like the parable, he would say, some seeds fall by the wayside, others on rocky ground or among the thorns. But it takes more than good ground (or as the Bible says understanding); it takes the proper climatic and environmental conditions, it takes luck. For it depends on chance, on adaptability, on strength. The railroads used herbicides, yet still some adventive plants survive. Why? How? It's like life, he would say to Juris, our life.

Received Ideas, Science 1988
Science is the search for the truth.
There is an objective truth independent of our observation that we are pursuing.
Everything is susceptible to the scientific method.
The scientific method is rational and logical.

And along with the metaphors, there was the implied imperative: flourish, contribute. Bear intellectual fruit.

Those first years in Alberta were not barren: Juris did some work, he gave papers. But by his own standards they were inconclusive, inadequate. He spent a couple of years attempting a physical separation of all the cells of the bone marrow. He worked compulsively, rigorously but got nowhere. He researched the transit of amino acids by lymphocytes and made some modest discoveries.

First this and then that, Juris cast about, anxious to produce. Meanwhile, Andrejs Zeps's name was becoming respected in the world of botany, needling Juris, even more than his injunction, into trying harder. Against all odds, with no support, his father had chosen a field of knowledge and made it his own. After seventy, he became an acknowledged expert in adventive plants and Latvian plants, with a string of articles and his encyclopedia published in the U.S. Even after his death his stature grew. With the new thaw, his encyclopedia was about to appear in Latvia. The new section of the botanical gardens in the city where Juris had been a displaced boy and his parents thick-tongued foreigners, these gardens were being named in honor of Andrejs Zeps. He achieved so much. How could Juris not measure himself against him? And he, as his father used to remind him, he had it so easy. He had a lab, equipment, bright assistants, the weight of the university, all buoying him up, assuring his place in the community of scientists.

When Juris remembered his father, he remembered him alone. He saw him walking away down the railroad track: his grey head bent, his shoulders stooped, his leg trailing, his eyes alert. He saw him at his desk, peering through a magnifying glass to read. And with the memory, Juris reminded himself that he had to go beyond what Andrejs did, beyond the nineteenth century to something revolutionary, to something that would make a difference.

INTERRUPTION

Nietzsche once claimed that Flaubert's disease came from too much sitting down. Great minds, he thought, need movement and open air. And there is something perverse, I think as I sit at the computer, about the writing life. Outside, hesitant Northern spring shades into brief and precious summer. The scent of flowering Mayday and lilac trail through the open window. I should not be sitting here, staring at the pulsating screen, hours and days reduced to a waste of confused thoughts. I should be out walking, smelling, feeling, before we are caught by winter again.

Daughter number one calls. She needs a specific brand of shimmery ballet tights for rehearsal tomorrow. The first and second dance shops I try are sold out in her size. By the time I find the tights in a mall across town and return to the computer, I am tired and must begin supper. I must face it; sitting too long at the computer is the least of my problems.

Why has my Emma not chosen the artistic life? She is talented and educated. Why does she not believe that she on her own can produce the magic she made in collaboration with Jack Nadow? The questions are simple. The answers, as always, are complicated, as complicated and contradictory as experience. And the narratives I imagine, my version of the answers, seem sentimental or false. I hit the delete button, and when that's too slow I blacken out pages, click, gone, back to the void.

What do I know for certain? I do remember the atmosphere of the times. No one ever came straight out and said that a woman could not be an artist. But when the artistic process was described, the terms used were masculine: virile, courageous, powerful, potent, brawny, active. Painters were adventurers, matadors, heroes doing battle on and with the canvas. The abstract painters were referred to as serious men, and no one bothered to mention that some of them were female. Serious men. Emma wanted to make lithographs and prints, but she didn't feel that she was serious enough or strong enough or American enough or original enough. She was trained to appreciate the full extent of the achievement of Western art. How could she ever expect to add to it?

I do remember all the emphasis on the great, the best, of the past and present. Either you were born a genius or you were not. If you were not, social and historical circumstances, encouragement, success, luck or possible audience, mattered. If you were, you would produce the great work, no matter what, and you would – no matter what – be recognized. Genius will out. Now it's easy to see I was given and believed not an immutable truth but an idea I can classify and dismiss: an idea that originated in German Romanticism. It's easy to see because over twenty years have passed. Now we hold other ideas as truths. Twenty years from now, we will classify and dismiss. Though wouldn't it be useful if we could judge the ideas that shape our lives as we live them?

Daughter number two is invited to a birthday party at exactly the same time of daughter number one's Spanish dance class. The events are at two ends of the city. I planned to work; instead both my husband and I hit the freeways.

Oddly enough it was through Flaubert, the great male writer of the realistic novel, Flaubert, the giant of French literature, that I began to look skeptically upon the theories of genius. Gustav compared the writing of a book to the building of a pyramid, "hoisting great blocks one atop another by dint of sheer brute strength, time and sweat." And I am struck, reading the details of his life, how much he did work. The words did not flow easily from his pen. Four months on the twenty-seven-page scene at the agricultural fair, a week on a paragraph, hours on a sentence. His books, he claimed, were indicative of patience not genius, labour not talent.

To write, one needs time, effort, and concentration – and not the divine touch. I take courage and hope from Flaubert's example. I might be limited, but I can work, I will work. After all, over a century has passed since Emma Bovary lived her wretched story. Twenty years of feminism separate me from the masculine cant of my college years. Today, Emma could tell her own story; today, she could be the teller, not the told. I pick up my battered and worn copy of *Madame Bovary*. I sit down at my desk. I whisper to myself: *Flaubert, c'est moi.*

Though still I am left with a niggling doubt. His metaphor of the pyramid has such masculine overtones. *"Sheer brute strength."* And when I imagine the building, I see gangs of slaves toiling. There is more here than I want to face. Time, effort, and enslavement? Does the writing life bring bondage to an idea? Or, at least, a shackling to the computer?

Received Ideas, Edmonton 1992
You can only tell your own story, no one else's.
The only truth is that there is none.
Formalism ensures boredom.
Pluralism is essential; still we should all
sound/write/sing the same.

IV

Emma and Juris were in the Saab on their way to the president's barbecue where Juris was being honoured again for his diabetic research.

"You should have said we'd be out of town." She was staring into the mirror on the sunflap making sure her mascara hadn't smudged.

"This is good politics, going to these things."

"They're such a bore. I nearly died last month at that dinner. The speeches were bad enough, if I hear one more word about the north, I'll scream. And then I had to make nice with all those earnest wives."

"Frances and Jerome are going to be there."

"Woop dee doo."

"It's a lovely evening. It'll be pleasant outside."

"If we don't get eaten by mosquitos."

"We should have walked."

"I couldn't. Not in these heels. Anyway, you said we had to rush." Emma smiled suddenly. "Andrejs's bugs would escape just as we were about to leave. I love scrambling for roaches in my best clothes."

"That wasn't chance. Michael took the aquarium lid."

"The monkey! On purpose? Did you speak to him?"

"He played innocent. But I found the lid in his underwear drawer."

"Yuck. Still, circumstantial evidence."

"It was him. But I didn't tell Andy. He's too quick with the fists lately."

"Absolutely. Michael was probably revenging himself for that bruise on his shoulder."

"Neverending warfare."

"Like most things."

Juris and Emma were standing on the sidewalk beside

the just parked Saab. Together, they looked across the broad lawn before them to the house and garden overflowing with people and noise.

"Here we go," Emma said, without moving.

"You look nice," Juris said.

"Really?" She turned back to the car and checked her reflection in the window. She smoothed out her blouse's broad, lace trimmed collar. Then, she touched the amber brooch at her throat. "I don't know if. . . ."

"I think I see Frances," Juris said.

With a last look, Emma turned away from the car and began to follow her husband up the walk.

"Be polite," he said.

"Yes, Daddy. Whatever you say, Daddy. Look, I don't mind Frances and Jerome. Really. She's so sweet and well meaning in her tight-assed way. Not that you can ever see her ass. Ah yes, look at that, another long-skirted, treacly flowered jumper. Forty going on fifteen. I told her she needs a new wardrobe. . . ." Lowering her voice as they approached the shiny president and his shiny wife at the entrance to the shiny brick house, Emma switched targets. "Here we are. Mr. Headache remedy and Mrs. Sometimes washing isn't enough."

"Emma!" Juris grabbed her arm though she had already put on a smile.

The university president, silver haired, smooth faced, greeted them with an firm, deep voice. "Dr. Zeps and Mrs. Zeps, Juris and Aida, such a pleasure." He shook Juris's hand. "And you are finally receiving some of the recognition you deserve."

The wife was a modest echo. "Wonderful. . . please . . . make yourselves . . . buffet . . . refreshments. . . ."

A few steps from the official welcome, Frances and Jerome waited. "Why hello there," Emma said. "What a surprise."

Jerome leaned over his cane. "Very nice, Emma. Quite smashing."

Frances looked at Emma's legs and said, "I wore the mini in the sixties, which convinces me I'm too old to wear it now."

"We'll get the wine," Juris said. "White, all right?" The men headed for the bar. By the time they returned, glasses in each hand, Frances was launched into a detailed description of Ian's brilliance. And how she was considering sending Katherine away to St. Michael's. There's no money spent here on exceptional children, only on the "challenged." And it is so important that they receive a proper foundation. How else will they be able to compete? How else will they find a place in the future?

> In England –
> Or even in the prep schools down east –
> Uniforms, instead of silly designer label –
> Umm, Emma said.
> I think Andy takes after his grandfather, she said.
> I need more wine, she said.

Juris's feet were in the Emma – Jerome – Francis circle, but his head was angled away. He was deep in conversation with the elderly looking physics professor beside him.

Starved, Emma said. And she went off in the direction of the buffet tables only to take a sudden right to the bar. Sipping watery wine and contemplating where to head next, she saw a few feet away a dark haired woman in flowing robes. Emma smiled and took a step towards her. Last year she had spent a pleasant evening in conversation with this woman who was, if Emma remembered correctly, an English professor much interested in contemporary art. "Maria Cristina," Emma raised her voice. "Hello." The woman did not respond. She continued to stare, her face blank, in Emma's direction. Had she forgotten who Emma was? Was she simply pretending not to see her? Or was Maria Cristina not her name? Emma could feel herself beginning to flush.

"How's the walking going?" said a voice at her ear. It was him – the runner – with his jaw and his shoulders (under an Italian suit) and, what's more, close up he had neon blue eyes and a lemony-vanilla smell that washed over her in a heart quickening wave. Looking away, pulling herself together before she spoke, Emma glanced again at Maria Cristina. The woman was still looking at her, or was it him, but now her face was pulled into an expression of distaste.

"I haven't seen you running for a while," Emma said.

"I've been away. Business."

"Toronto?"

"LA. New York. . . ."

The string quartet had stopped playing. Dr. Dapper, the president, perched on the back step, was calling for attention. On his right were Juris and a blond man, whose picture Emma had seen in the paper on the occasion of his winning an international prize for his research in ecology. The other guests were obediently gathering into a semicircle. Emma and her friend did not move. "Should you be up there?" she asked. "Are you being honoured?"

"I'm no professor. I'm Robert Lamartine," he said, pronouncing his name in the French way. He obviously expected her to have heard of him, which she had, though she couldn't remember the context. She shook his hand, and when she started to pull away, he held on. "And who are you?"

"I'm Emma Zeps. My husband's getting an award. For his research. Well, he got it already, but they're going to mention it. . . ."

"On this glorious midsummer evening, I would like to welcome everyone . . . our distinguished board, honoured colleagues and friends. . . ." Dr. Dapper began.

Robert Lamartine finally dropped her hand. "I'm on the distinguished board."

"Sounds dull," Emma said.

"Sometimes. I'm used to it."

The chancellor, introduced as one of Edmonton's most prominent lawyers and its foremost philanthropist, had taken Dapper's place. "Not a hundred years ago this was all untouched wilderness," he was saying. "Impenetrable forests, teeming rivers, raw nature. . . ."

"You're in law?" Emma said.

And Robert Lamartine laughed and took a step closer. "Business. Little of this. Little of that."

The chancellor was working his way through the fur trade, the fort, transportation systems, and the birth of the city.

"So you had no fun on this trip of yours?" Emma asked, gazing into Robert's eyes.

"I wouldn't say that." He blinked frequently. She could see the blue contact lenses floating on his eyes.

"Where did you stay in New York?"

"The Plaza." Emma saw an ornate, gold stencilled room, an enormous white meringue bed, a room service cart with silver domed plates and crystal champagne glasses. "We had a wonderful meal the first night at a place on the Brooklyn side. Fantastic view. Water Cafe, I think it was called." Emma saw him with a beautiful woman, lit by candlelight, the Manhattan skyline as backdrop.

The chancellor was extolling the city of festivals, gateway to the north, city of champions, a vibrant, alive place . . . home to a *world class* university.

"The next night we saw the *Phantom of the Opera*."

"How touristy of you." Emma smiled to soften the

effect of her words. "It has a certain charm, but it's not my New York. I'd stay at Morgan's or the Royalton. I'd have dinner at the Canal Bar or Lucky Strike. And I'd go to see something off Broadway, or maybe the Mark Morris Dance Company. I'd love to see him dance Dido."

"You would, would you," Robert said in an affectionate tone, Emma thought, an intimate tone.

Dr. Dapper was back on the podium. He spoke of the city within the city, 30,000 constituents, world class professors, world class institution . . . on the cutting edge. . . .

"Boost, boost, boost. If it really was world class, they wouldn't have to say it was," Emma said with a head gesture towards Dapper.

"Reassuring us and himself."

"Nurturing the life of the mind," the president said.

"It's not working." Robert's hand had landed ever so gently on her back.

Her back answered with goosebumps. Embarrassed, Emma began to edge away, around the respectful throng to the buffet table.

"Unfortunately, years of cutbacks are endangering the fabric of this intellectual community. . . ."

Robert followed.

Still, there had been continuing excellence in the face of budgetary restraints. "That is why we are all gathered together here, tonight, to celebrate the achievements of two of our most respected colleagues. Dr. Zeps, Juris, and . . ."

"This is same old stuff too," Robert said, looking over the cheeses, pâtés and breads.

"their contribution to the world-wide community of scholars. . . ."

"I'm famished," Emma said, picking up a plate.

"Dr. Zeps – in the battle against one of mankind's

most devastating, most persistent diseases. . . ."

I could be talking of all the battles he's avoided, Emma thought, knowing that she was being unfair. Of all that he hasn't done. She leaned over to cut a hunk of Brie. As she straightened, Robert held a strawberry to her mouth. In surprise, she pulled back. He pushed. The fruit butted her lips until she opened and bit into the fleshy sweetness.

Science is trial and error with notes.

In all the Latvian folk arts – ceramics, woodcraft, metal, and fibre arts – certain ancient symbols are used.

The sign of *Mara* is a zigzag line.

The sign of *Diveturi*, the ancient faith, is the cross of crosses.

The sign of Moon is an open square on an angle.

The sign of *Saule* is an eight-segmented circle that resembles a stylized flower.

"I saw you," Frances said to Emma, "talking to that horrible man." They were in Mayfair Park at the playschool's year-end picnic. Both of them had driven a carload of children, both had brought food, Frances – raw vegetables and dip, Emma – chocolate-iced donuts.

"Horrible man? Who do you mean?" Emma asked, looking at the food she was laying out and not at Frances.

"You know. At the president's do? Lamartine. You seemed very well acquainted."

"Do you know him?" Emma asked, eager for any details.

"Mostly by reputation."

"It's bad?"

"Don't you remember when the 114th Street road widening kerfuffle started? He led the fight to close Keillor Road because the traffic was bothering him. I went over with a couple of others from the neighbourhood. He wouldn't even listen to what we had to say. I'm not interested, he said, and he ushered us out. Took me by the elbow and pushed. He's rude and he's arrogant."

"Is he married?"

"Can you wait a minute, sweetie pie," Frances said to a curly-haired little girl who had snuck past them and was grabbing a donut. "Wait till Shaun's Mum has opened the juice? Besides, those are for dessert." Then, noticing Janie coming towards them, "She knows Mr. Lamartine, I think."

"*Ciao*, peoples," Janie said, plonking herself down on the grass at their feet. "I've done my bit for the grade twos." She spread her legs in a V and bent her upper body down over the right one.

"Frances says you know Robert Lamartine."

"Umm." She switched legs. "I met him when I worked on that AIDS evening. He does a lot for different charities. I'll say that for him. But not much else. He's too full of himself. Frances, I've been waiting and waiting for a plumber...."

"What do you mean," Emma interrupted Janie, "full of himself?"

"Don't you read the papers? That steel plant strike last year? That was him. He owns the plant. As I was saying, everything's ready to be hooked up. Except for the taps. They haven't arrived. So I wondered, Frances, could you give me the phone number of the guy you use? I'm sick of washing dishes in the bathtub."

"Is Lamartine married?" Emma asked. "Do you know where his offices are?"

Emma waited and waited. For what? A sign from him. A sign from Juris. Any sign as to what she must do. She was suspended, waiting, like Sleeping Beauty or Snow White, suspended, alive, but still: still in her house, still hungry for something other than, as the song went, her "daily loaves of dread." She was no longer depressed or no longer as depressed. She thought everything soon will be different. When the doorbell rang, she expected a delivery man with a box of long stemmed roses. When the phone rang, she expected to hear his voice on the line. But when she opened the door, when she picked up the phone, her expectations were never fulfilled. Would her magic moment never come? Would this spell never be broken?

She did see Lamartine along the drive but from far off. He seemed always to be running in the same direction she was, but ahead, hundreds of metres ahead. She pushed herself; she willed her legs to move faster and faster, but she never caught up. Once she had just started her walk when she looked up to see him – finally – running towards her. He did not slow down. As he passed, he smiled and nodded. That was all. Her hello, her sudden joy, dried and caked on her lips.

The inconstant Moon is male.

The all important Sun is female.

Since the Sun dominates the heavens, her sign, the eight segmented circle is used more than all the other signs in Latvian design.

After that, he disappeared from the drive. Day after day, she came back from her walks heavy-hearted. She was short-tempered with the boys. She snapped at Juris.

"You're so dense, sometimes."

Juris shrugged, "I just asked if you could iron me a shirt

before I leave tonight. I have to wear something in Washington. I explained how important this trip is. If I get this grant . . . it could make the difference."

"Iron it yourself."

"I'm busy. I said . . . I have to pack, organize my material. Please. Emma. Do I ask so much?"

"I'll go buy you a new one. How's that? A good luck shirt."

She grabbed her keys. "Mum – " Michael tackled her on her way to the door. He hung onto her knees. "You said you'd read to me. You promised."

She detached him, finger by finger. She pushed him away. And as she did, she felt amazed by what she was doing. Be-witched. She'd been turned into the wicked queen. Face it, you are definitely not the fairest of them all, she told herself on the way out the door. Witch, she said to her reflection in the rearview mirror, as she checked her hair and lipstick.

She backed the car out of the garage, and instead of taking the direct way to Southgate, up 76th Avenue, she turned left and went north on Saskatchewan Drive. She slowed when she passed Lamartine's house. He must be away. It was nearly a week. Was he on holiday with his wife? The two of them sailing around the Mediterranean on a yacht. She could imagine. Rome. Paris. It was frightening how vividly she could imagine.

But imagination was not knowledge. And Emma couldn't bear not knowing. She couldn't bear how opaque, how impenetrable his life was to her, both a dark presence that she circled hopelessly and a dark absence, a gap, at her emotional centre.

Each time she drove anywhere, even to the I.G.A., Emma drove by his house. Andy began to joke about "Mum's detour." "Concentrate on the view," Emma said.

"I'm exposing you to the splendour of the river valley," she said.

If she was alone, she sometimes parked a house or two away and watched. She watched a woman – a wife – bronzed skin and frosted hair, drive up in a BMW 325i; she watched Lamartine drive off in a Mercedes 450 SEL, watched them arrive and leave together. She saw a maid service car on Mondays and a gardener's truck on Tuesdays. One hot July day, as she sat under a pine tree, an older couple walking a Samoyed stared at her suspiciously. Had they spotted her before? She had to be discreet, inconspicuous.

"You must have had lessons in surveillance," she asked Janie, who had confessed after several bottles of wine at a dinner party that in pre-Edmonton, pre-children days she and Steve were in Intelligence.

"What?" Janie looked totally shocked. "What do you mean?"

"You know. In your CIA days. Did they teach you how to follow someone without being seen? Or, if you're watching a house. Is it best to lie down in a car? I need the whole routine. Anything you can remember."

"Why? What are you up to?"

"I asked first."

"It's not the way you think. Oh, Steve did decoding when he was in the army. You know how good he is with puzzles. Mathematical mind. During basic training they figured out what he'd be most useful as. Thank heavens. He was spared Vietnam. Then, later when he was doing his research for his thesis in East Africa: well, we both kept our eyes open. Made some reports. I don't know why I said anything. I must have been pie-eyed."

"You were."

"And you've harboured this for two years?"

"I didn't dwell on it. I found it interesting. Like what you told me about all the women around here being on tranquillizers. Or the Reeses, did I tell you, hiring an architect to design their garage? To be sure standards are maintained, she told me. . . . In a bloody garage."

"I don't see the connection."

"Examples of how behind these conventional, mild-mannered exteriors there lurks aberration. And weirdness."

"You've changed."

"I've found my true role model – Mrs. Peel. Don't look so mystified. Emma Peel, in "The Avengers." I think I need a catsuit to dash around in. And they're so fashionable too. Do you think I could carry it off? Or should I diet first?"

"You seem less depressed. A bit hyper though. What's happened?"

Emma wanted to tell Janie everything. She longed to be able to dwell on the meagre details, to give voice to her morass of feelings. But seeing Janie's trim, disciplined body spread out on the sofa, watching her bounce one bony knee, she knew she should say nothing. "I'm into self-improvement. I've got a babysitter, and I'm thinking of getting the broken veins on my legs zapped."

INTERRUPTION

Of all her impulsive, thoughtless acts, I find I can least forgive Emma Bovary her treatment of her daughter: her thrusting Berthe away so violently that she falls against the bureau, her neglect, her lack of love and care. When Emma ruins herself and Charles, she blights Berthe's future, condemns her to working in a cotton mill, condemns her to poverty and toil.

I can't forgive her, but I understand too well that sudden, overwhelming irritation that jerks her arm out, pushing her little girl away. I don't push, but I snap, I screech, I whine. I evade my duties for an hour here or there. My writing, I say with self-importance. I need to write I declare, trying to convince and pacify myself.

Flaubert, *c'est moi.* I repeat the phrase insistently. Flaubert, *c'est moi.* It is my mantra: my ritual invocation of power to transform, to be transformed. (Gustave himself spoke of wanting not the fame of Corneille: "But to be Corneille! To feel *oneself* Corneille.") To feel *myself* Flaubert? Even the shape of his days is an object of my desire.

When Flaubert was working on *Madame Bovary*, he would awaken about ten in the morning. Until his bell rang, no one in the household was allowed to speak louder than a whisper or to make other noise. Once his bell rang, a servant brought him the mail, the newspaper, a glass of water, and a filled pipe. His mother came to sit on his bed, while he smoked and read for about an hour. He then would get dressed and go down for a meal that combined breakfast and lunch. Afterwards he would stroll and smoke in the company of the rest of the family, on the terrace or by the wide river. From one to two he gave his niece Caroline lessons in history or mythology and from two till dinner at seven, he worked in his study. About nine or ten, he began again, working until two or three in the morning. On Sunday nights he would read aloud what he had written during the week to Louis Bouilhet, his closest friend.

> Together they read over sentences dozens, even hundreds, of times; and then, when each sentence seemed right, they read over the paragraphs into which they were combined.
>
> Francis Steegmuller

Emma continued to drive by the Lamartine house. In the daytime, she no longer stopped. She was afraid of being seen. Besides, she had learned the very little she could learn watching the coming and goings. At night, dressed from head to foot in dark clothes, she would stand in the back alley (often pressed against a tree) and watch for fifteen minutes at a time. She could see slices of rooms: ceilings, parts of walls, two moving figures, all lit up, as if under floodlights: a play of a perfect modern marriage. To see more clearly, she brought opera glasses, and closer-up the backdrop was marred. The furniture and the art were both conventional: pretty and undistinguished, chintzy sofas, imitation Chinese tables, too-sweet flower watercolours and Southwest art ripoffs. I could have done better, Emma thought, if I'd been choosing instead of her.

She wanted to see more than flickering shadows on a cave wall. She wanted to break through the plate glass that enclosed his magazine perfect life, that enclosed her recumbent self in a passive princess pose. She wanted to taste and touch.

Mrs. Peel would never have just stood and watched; she was intrepid, prepared for what came, be it sword fights or crocodiles. Not that she would have been interested in a mystery such as Robert Lamartine. She would have dismissed him with one knowing look.

In the Latvian card game *Zolite*, the Queen, not the King is the top card. Queens always beat out Kings.

The next night, a Sunday night, Emma brought a flashlight. Monday was blue box pickup. All the recyclables were out. *The Globe and Mail, The Financial Post, Canadian Business Weekly, Fortune, Town and Country,* and *Architectural Digest* (what *arriviste* taste the woman had). Six skim milk cartons, one oat bran box, two frozen pizza boxes, four crumpled diet coke cans, a Chivas Regal bottle, a California White Zinfandel (wouldn't you know it) and, inside a Reebok Pumps box, a pile of broken glass ampules and still another box, a cobalt blue one marked LaPrairie Treatment, bearing a price tag of $270.

The next night, Emma was hungrier, bolder. She'd taught herself to step cautiously, soundlessly. In the house, only one light was on, in the right back bedroom. A perky TV theme floated from the open window. The evening was warm, and in her excitement Emma was sweating. She rolled up her blouse sleeves and unbuttoned her top two buttons. She pulled on a pair of thin plastic gloves, then lifted the lid to the first garbage can. Though the plastic bag was closed, trickles of fishy stink dampened her resolve. She dropped the lid, causing a small clatter. Think of what you could discover, she chided herself.

And as she stood beside the garbage cans, preparing herself, she heard a car turning into the alley. The headlights approached slowly. She pressed herself against a tree. The lights passed the only garage on the alley. Emma waited, her heart stuttering. The lights stopped a few feet away. Searching for relief from the unforgiving brightness, she rested her face on the scratchy tree bark. "Get in." It was Juris's voice. He was standing, a faceless shadow behind the opened car door. "Emma – "

She obeyed, walking around to the passenger side. When she sat, she tucked her gloved hands under her thighs. How was she going to get them off without his noticing? Perhaps, if she edged her right hand over until a finger reached her left wrist? And tugged. She had to keep her weight off her thighs and balance on her toes, in order to have room to manoeuver. She dropped it then pushed it under the seat with her heel. She must look odd, hunched over. Thank goodness, he wasn't looking at her. He was driving as if he were alone in the car. In the dim light, she could see only the outline, the presence of his face. She had the other glove. She dropped it and straightened.

"It was a nice night. I needed a walk." To her own ears, she sounded artificial. "You know how I am. I get curious about houses." She had to take a breath every couple of words.

Did he believe her? Had it been coincidence that he'd come down that alley? Surely not. He must have known where she was. And if he knew that. . . . Would it be better to come clean? Wouldn't he respect her more if she was honest? She would talk to him; she should talk to him. It would be such a relief to share it with him. And hadn't he always put things in perspective for her? Point it out for me, she'd joke: foreground, background, vanishing point. I can't see it. And he would. Even if often she rejected his detached vision, argued for alternatives. Talk, she told herself.

But her tongue lay inert, weighed down by stones of fear.

Juris drove into their garage. He turned off the motor, removed the key. The automatic light dimmed and went off. "You left the kids alone." His voice was flat with anger. "I got back from the lab. And I found them alone. No sign of you."

For a second, the words still would not come. Then, she managed: "They were asleep. Anyway, Andy's not a baby anymore."

"This must never happen again."

"I needed a walk."

"I've been patient. All through the winter. I was relieved when you seemed to pick up. I didn't know there would be new ... problems."

"I didn't plan it. Or will it. Juris, let's go in." She was thinking that in their bedroom her hands would not feel so heavy. She would be able to reach out and draw him into the comfort and reassurance of familiar pleasure. She opened her door. "Juris – "

He did not move. He stared straight ahead into the darkness. "I'm going back to the lab."

Science is trial and error with notes.

Traditionally, as a matter of course, paintings have used both plane and recession as methods of organization. In primitive art, recession is ignored. In abstract art, recession is destroyed; all is plane, all is surface, all is flat. Now think of plane as the present, recession as the past.

Look to where you are going, her professor said, not from where you come.

Received Ideas, Chicago 1972
Make Love not war.
Do your own thing.
It's all a question of taste.
Get in touch with your feelings.

When Juris first met Emma, she was infatuated with her professor. Juris and Emma were both at the University of Chicago. He was doing postgraduate work; she was working on her M.A. in Art History. But they met not under the gothic arches of the campus, not in one of the many student bars, or at a party at a faculty house in Hyde Park; no, they met miles away in a row house on the near-north side (on Lincoln and Madison).

Once a month Juris drove across the city to have dinner "as your poor Mama would have made it" with Aunt Ruta, an elderly woman who was not an aunt but a cousin of Juris' mother. She lived alone; she had lost everyone except a daughter, who had recently married but – thank the Lord – at least lived in the neighbourhood. "You should be thinking of settling down," she would say to Juris over the crispy oven potatoes, the beets, and the pork roast.

"Wonderful food," he would answer. "I needed this. I tend to survive on burgers and fries cause I'm so busy. Just another slice."

Out of respect, he never told Aunt Ruta how her cooking was not at all like his mother's. Mama had cooked only because it was necessary. She could not bear to touch flesh or fish. With a long handled fork, she speared pieces of meat and dropped them into the frying pan. She boiled vegetables until they were limp and soggy. "Think of what has touched this carrot," she'd say. She insisted that the smell of food cooking made her feel ill. Each meal was a sacrifice she made for the survival of her husband and son. Juris took to opening cans and making sandwiches at a young age.

"I am seeing a girl," he confessed finally, after Aunt Ruta went on and on about finding the right girl for him. "She's an assistant in the lab. Very bright. Very serious. From Deerborn, Michigan." On his next visit, he found Emma sitting on the couch, her yellow hair framed by embroidered pillows. Emma, who had never been in the habit of letting herself be introduced to nice, Latvian boys, was as surprised by his presence as he was by hers. Fortunately, she was amused rather than angry. And though he was half-heartedly engaged to be married to his sincere assistant and wholeheartedly engaged in a physical relationship with her, and though he resented Ruta's setting him up, he was taken with Emma: the way her laughter erupted from deep inside her, the way her grey eyes lit up when she spoke. Her fluent Latvian, and her figure in her short, tight black dress, these too took him, led him into new territory.

Unlike his previous visits, they ate at the dining room table with a white cloth and candles. There was a bottle of wine, a good French Bordeaux, that Emma had brought. The two of them, Aunt Ruta begging off, drank it down in head spinning time. He must have spoken of his plans, his present research, Chicago and New York. Afterwards he couldn't remember a word he said.

What Emma said, he did remember. She talked of her graduate studies and her professor, the famous Roth.

"He challenges me," she said, her eyes full of light. "He makes me examine all my. . . ," she hesitated, then used English, ". . . all my preconceptions." She flipped back into Latvian. "He's taught me to think before I speak or write. I thought I was pretty smart. I thought I knew. But he's made me see. I handed in this paper I was so proud of. He called it bullshit – to my face." She smiled. "And it was. Yes. Others would have given up. But I recognized his brilliance and decided it was worth hanging on." She leaned across the table. "I'm learning to be critical, to judge." She was speaking English again. "To understand what's central and what's marginal, central to the development, the history of art. What's inevitable. We share a dedication to American art, to a new aestheticism and formalism, a new search for pure form."

Juris hadn't known what she was talking of, but over the next few months he learned. He met the great professor Roth, a tall man, a big man, with a large, droopy mustache, a sprawling presence and an abstract vocabulary. "Can't you feel the weight of his intelligence?" Emma asked, and Juris did not answer. Roth was a member of the most prestigious interdisciplinary organization on campus, The Committee on Social Thought. "The whole group – as solid and well, heavy, as the stones of these buildings. I mean when I say heavy, these guys are *heavy*." For, Roth had also taken Emma up (though not, unlike Juris, taken up with her). She was the favourite, the anointed one, taken to cocktail parties to be introduced to the likes of Bellow and Arendt.

If Juris resented her invoking the name of Roth at every opportunity, he was also intrigued by that other culture, the world of elite art that was her milieu. Emma was such a relief after the women he'd known before: the secretary and the model, both pretty, pleasing and dense, or the university girls, all of them too earnest, too left wing.

"I know," Emma giggled, after pressing him for details of his now discarded girlfriend. "Short hair and Birkenstocks. Am I right? Marches against the war once a week? I went to college with these righteous girls. I know."

She did know the tone he was comfortable with. It was often hers. They shared assumptions, and, in the proper sense, they shared a history.

"Tonight, you're not allowed to mention Roth."

"Who says?"

"Each time you pronounce his name, I win a forfeit," Juris insisted.

"Don't play tough with me."

He hung on.

Emma Avendemis at twenty-two: the face was still more Aida than Emma, the skin young, translucent, glowing. Full makeup was pale lipstick and black eyeliner. When she sat with Juris in the diner, discussing the movie they had just seen, she would pull her long hair off her face by running her fingers up through the crown, exposing her high forehead, and letting it fall in a graceful swoop back over her shoulders. She had a habit, if she was excited, of cutting him off, letting her words tumble out, one almost knocking the other down. Conversely, if he was explaining something about his work, one night it was the spinning out of genetic lines, she would hesitate, examine his face, start to form a word, pause again and only then speak.

Emma Zeps at thirty-eight: now she was truly Emma. Her face had lost that touch of youthful softness, of roundness; her nose looked sharper. There were faint lines around her eyes, and on her depressed days creases ran from her nostrils to the corners of her mouth. Full makeup was more subtle and more extensive: shadow, foundation, powder, and mascara: camouflage. Dancing with Robert Lamartine at the art gallery fundraiser, she looked pink and gold beautiful, glittering droplets cascading from ears to bare shoulders. She looked remote, her chin up, her eyes not meeting his.

She had joined his favourite charity as a volunteer, wooed not his wife (no, she avoided her) but a couple of women in their circle, wooed them into social acquaintance, so she could easily know where the Lamartines planned to be. She had schemed and she had plotted, but when he sought her out for a dance, when he was suddenly not just a fantasy but a reality, his flesh touching hers, she was nearly overcome. She held herself tightly, tightly. Her stomach and her heart were fluttering; her hand in his was damp with sweat.

Close up, he was crisper, shinier, than her image of him, his clothes, his hair, his nails, so clean-edged that the other men on the dance floor appeared slightly blurred in comparison. His was the style, the gleam, of money.

He put his mouth to her ear. "Have lunch with me. Tomorrow."

For a second, the ghost of Aida, wondering, tremulous, was visible around her eyes and in the set of her mouth. "What?"

"Lunch. Tomorrow."

INTERRUPTION

Emma Zeps. Can you see her as she smiles and gazes into Lamartine's eyes?

Emma Bovary. There's no need to ask. Flaubert lets us all see and know his Emma.

> Every time she played a card, the movement lifted her dress on the right side. From her coiled hair, a dark glow ran down her back, paling gradually until it merged into shadow. As she sat back again, her dress puffed out on either side of her, in full folds that reached to the floor.

Flaubert, c'est moi? Each time I pick up *Madame Bovary* again, I feel how unapproachable he is, the god-like author he wanted to be, everywhere present and nowhere visible. *Flaubert, c'est moi?* Get real, as my Emma would say.

This question of a model, of a literary forefather, is tricky. I contemplate another kind of author, another kind of authority, a foremother rather than a forefather. If Flaubert's cloak is itchy, ill-fitting, the colour too murky for my complexion. I will imagine myself in a white, high-waisted dress. My hair up.

To feel myself Austen?

I do not envy her life: the way she had to humble herself and bend her will to that of others. Flaubert created a heroine who (since she is a woman in the provinces) has fewer possibilities than he did, whose life will be a long, narrow corridor with a shut door at the end. In contrast, Austen's Emma, though boxed in with nothing to do, still has more open to her than her author. When Austen wrote Emma, she had neither Emma's fortune nor her youth.

1. Flaubert's household revolved around his rhythms, his needs, his work.
   Austen catered to the needs of others; no one catered to her. She would interrupt her writing, hiding her work when visitors arrived or a servant entered the room.

2. Flaubert had a study at Croisset with tall, mahogany bookcases, a sofa, and a large round writing table, with three windows onto the garden and two onto the everchanging spectacle of the Seine and its boats.
   Austen had no room of her own; she shared her bedroom with her sister and had to write in a corner of a crowded living room on a small round table.

3. He travelled to Egypt, Nubia, the mid-East, a trip into the exotic, the alien, the unknown. He looked upon eunuchs; he visited brothels and Cairo bathhouses. He was able to experience as much of the hidden and the forbidden as he desired.
   Austen travelled very little; she experienced very little.

4. Though he lost his fortune eventually through mismanagement and extravagance, he was financially independent for most of his life. He never had to work at a job to support himself.
   She remained unmarried and unprovided for – a poor relation.

5. Flaubert's mother treated him with affection and respect. She encouraged and supported his writing.
   Her mother did not hover over her; rather she sent her off whenever she could – at birth to a wet nurse, at six to boarding school. Even when she was ill, at the end of her short life, she could not lie on the sofa; it was reserved

for her mother. She had to make do with three chairs
pushed together.

Foremother or forefather?

Although Flaubert had a much more enviable life than Austen, there is one choice he made that I would not want to repeat. He sacrificed everything for his art: friendship, health, the possibility (the satisfaction) of a wife or child. I have trouble sacrificing anything. I want it all. "Fuck your inkwell," he advised a young writer, which strikes me as a more useful metaphor for a male writer than a female, unless the inkwell is unusually shaped. I want it all. *Jouissance* of the text is not enough for me. I need the real thing.

Received Ideas, Edmonton 1992
If you aren't part of the solution, you're part of the problem.
If you're female, you can't have it all.
(You can . . .)
       Have a nice day.
        Take care.
            Have a good life.   (But)
You can't have it all.

Emma's first lunch with Lamartine did not go as she hoped. He took her not to some intimate spot but to Earl's Tin Palace, mecca of middle management, hip but not the hippest. Then he let the hostess seat them at a plastic table outside in the bright, hot sun, so Emma was forced to squint to see his face clearly. After they ordered, he excused himself to make a long phone call. When he finally returned, his chicken fajita was growing cold. In answer to Emma's questions, he spoke of his past: his three years in the NHL until he was injured, his first moving company, his first car lot. But he spoke to her as if she were a reporter. He wasn't offering his history to her. Likewise, he questioned her on the facts, not the truth, of her life. And she – well, she had answered badly in half-phrases, all her wit gone.

Juris never mentioned or even alluded to the night he found Emma in Lamartine's alley. And she, in turn, put out of her mind the implication of his discovery. She did notice his hours at work were even longer than usual and his distracted air at home even deeper. He never seemed to start a conversation or to look at her. His eyes would slide over her face and fix somewhere else. And his lovemaking changed: it became abrupt, random, and for Emma, unpleasing. But that, Emma told herself, could be me rather than him.

Then Emma and Juris had their worst argument yet over her spending. Usually he did not open the bills as they arrived. He would let them pile up on his desk until the last day of the month when he sat down with checkbook in hand. This month, no matter how late he got home, he went looking for mail. He would rip open the envelopes, snort at the figures and shoot venomous looks at Emma.

"We're at the limit. Did I tell you last month? You have to control yourself."

"We're not quite at the limit, not on a couple of the cards," Emma answered placidly.

"What's this? Seventy-five dollars, Margo's florists?"

"Oh God, are you going to interrogate me now? It was for the fundraiser. I was reimbursed," Emma said, amused by how easily the lies popped into her mouth. Next time, she noted to herself, use cash, if there was any cash to be had, which since they were so overextended, wasn't likely. If Safeway didn't take Mastercard, we'd go hungry she once said to Frances, only partly for effect.

"And what about – ?"

"I refuse to do this." Emma was basking in the memory of the flowers, eighteen apricot-coloured, long stemmed roses. She had sent them anonymously after that first lunch with Lamartine in an attempt to reestablish the right mood. Naturally, he'd called the florist, who – as instructed – had refused to name names but had admitted yes, a woman, a tall, blonde woman.

Juris was searching for something, looking under tables, checking behind the sofa. "Refuse all you want," he said as he exited to the kitchen. Emma followed. He was at a drawer, fumbling. He pulled out a pair of shears. "You're going to have to start doing something useful."

She sat down. "I resent that." She gestured with her head towards the window that looked onto the yard where Michael and Harry were playing.

He still didn't look at her. "I meant out of this place."

"I have been. The volunteer work. And it's been good for me too."

"Look, I'm saying since you're gallivanting about day and night, you might as well start a job that earns something to pay off all these bills you keep running up." He put the shears on the table and walked past her to the hall.

"Gallivanting? What kind of word is that?" Emma raised her voice, so he would be able to hear her. "This isn't the nineteenth century. Gallivanting. Honestly Juris, what have you been reading lately? This doesn't suit you." Juris was back, carrying her purse. "What – " He unzipped the top, reversed it, and shook out the contents. "Have you gone crazy? How dare you?" She tried to collect a few bits and pieces – Kleenexes, pens, lipstick, mirror – and stuff them back in. He grabbed her wallet; she grabbed his wrist. "Give it back."

He ignored her. His mouth was tight, his expression determined. He pulled out a couple of charge cards. As he picked up the shears, she snatched back her wallet. "Juris," she said, "please." He cut each card in two and dropped the pieces into the garbage. "Give me the others."

"No way."

"No cards till you get a job."

"I can't believe this. A job?" Emma's mind went blank at the thought. "What could I? You want me to sling hash at a diner? I never learned to type, to word process, I guess they call it now. You know, computers give me the willies."

"You used to work."

"Freelance criticism. It's not easy to just waltz back in. I have no connections. Not here."

V

She found herself at the university, searching out the print studio, following arrows down grey cement corridors, up stairs, past knots of students that looked, in their jeans and miniskirts, remarkably like she and her group had looked almost twenty years before. Luckily she found the doors unlocked and the studio empty. She was able to wander. To smell the patch of spilled ink. To touch the stones lined up in a row under the expanse of sink. To inspect the metal presses. Not too much pressure and not too little. She remembered – a question of exactness, of care, a question of balance. Had that expertise all vanished?

There were several prints hung up to dry. Poorly drawn, she thought, muddy. Then, she smiled to herself – my trained eye, I haven't lost that. The doors opened to a ponytailed boy and a shorthaired girl. They were laughing, joking about a professor. As soon as they caught sight of Emma, they stopped. "Can I help you?" asked the girl.

"Just looking around," Emma said. Wondering, do my hands still know? Wondering, how much have I lost?

The Tree of Sun, which represents reaching upward and growth, uses several signs in its design. The Tree combines the signs for the Moon, the Earth, Fate and *Jumis*, prosperity.

As if in answer to her need, Lamartine phoned Emma and offered her a job as a graphic designer. "Part time," he said. "Pick your own hours."

Emma, who was washing last night's pots, pushed back her hair with a soapy hand. Was this a gift, she wondered, or a ploy? "I'm not trained in that kind of work."

"You couldn't do it?"

"I might be able to pick it up . . . after a bit."

"What are you trained to do?"

"To recognize and evaluate serious art. To explain what is good and what is important."

"Snob," he said.

Emma laughed, "No, you should call me old-fashioned: a dinosaur. If it comes to that."

She had no idea what he thought of her. He did call. They chatted when they met on Saskatchewan Drive. But she had no idea of his intentions, or even if he had intentions.

Kitsch imitates the effects of art.

He offered her another job, a short term one, to organize an art auction for medical research. Over lunch at the oak panelled dining room of the Centre Club, he introduced her to the rest of the steering committee. "She's the woman to do the job," he said. Emma blushed. The two men and three women gave her the once over.

Emma began to explain how difficult the job was going to be. "I don't know if it's possible. . . . Most of the artists in Edmonton are so poor they can't afford to donate. We could go outside of the city, of course. Hit some of the bigger names elsewhere." Too tense to eat, she picked at her salad as the others threw ideas around. Now and then, she came up with a suggestion: "Centrepieces that incorporate a miniature easel and paintbox. And one of the party favours could be a little tray of shadow and lipstick colours – to continue the paintbox theme. We could try MAC cosmetics. They're new and Canadian and might want to promote themselves."

"You've had some experience," the youngest of the men said to her.

Emma answered with a smile that she hoped said of course I do. She didn't want to admit that her knowledge of how these thing were done came from *Vogue*.

She felt something brush her leg above the knee. It grazed her upper thigh and landed on her crotch. She looked across the table at Lamartine. He was deep in conversation with the woman on his right. Had he stretched out his leg? Was it his foot? He looked so controlled, so cool, so distant. But who else? She wanted to look under the tablecloth, but she couldn't draw attention to what was going on. His toes burrowed busily into her vulva. Despite his socks, her pantyhose and panties, she felt a full repertoire of touches: tickling, massaging, stroking. What was he doing? It was so inappropriate. He'd never even kissed her. And now this. And with all these people around.

She dropped her hand to her lap and grabbed the big toe. He wrenched his foot away. He was watching her now, though still pretending to follow the back and forth of the discussion. His eyes spoke. . . . Why stop? Why?

We're in public, she thought.

This is embarrassing, she thought.

I am not at your disposal.

Yet her body had responded (to a foot), was still responding with a slippery, sliding flow of desire.

He would be her lover. Day and night, she dreamt of it. With her family or alone, she dreamt of it. Being borne away on the moment, borne away on a limitless stream of sensations, beyond restraint, beyond satisfaction, beyond all that she knew.

He would never be her lover. He was nothing to her: a crisp shirt, a clean jawline, an ingenious foot. Nothing.

She'd known men of intelligence, of substance, rocks not flotsam. She'd known Quality. Why would she be taken in by this facsimile? Not her. Certainly not. Why would she listen so avidly to his banalities? That was what was odd. How she not only listened but carried around his statements, reviewing them, rearranging them endlessly until they glowed, burnished by her attention, lit up by his will.

His 1,000-megawatt will. It was scrambling her currents of thought, overloading her circuits. High voltage, she thought, danger.

Beyond limits, she thought, beyond.

This was too probably her last chance. She already wasn't what she used to be. The years were speeding by. Soon, too soon, her breasts, her face would fall. She found three broken capillaries on her legs. See, she thought, age, the approaching end. She rushed to the dermatologist who inserted a tiny needle in the heart of each red cluster and flushed away the flaws, flushed away with salt and alcohol, warmth creeping up her leg. Gone, his needle a magic wand, except in a few minutes they were back, ugly and raw, and the actual erasure occurred slowly over several weeks.

Her new charge cards arrived just in time for her to buy a cream silk teddy, garter, stockings so light, so soft, better than being nude, she felt each breeze, each eddy of air. Driving into the country in his Mercedes, ice blue outside, dark blue inside, speeding through the perfect autumn day motor purring, Mozart playing, speeding to his land by a lake. Should I build, he asked, I've been thinking condo in Palm Springs, but a place at the lake is what they have here, what they have at home too.

The gold and red leaves scrunched under their feet. The

light was sharp and bright. Emma told a story on Frances and her homemade pinatas for school parties, hours and hours of work *(kiss me now)* she's crazy, and Halloween's coming, you won't believe the costumes *(now)* authentic fourteenth century ladies, it's a religion in Belgravia *(what's wrong)* honour the child and his whims. Robert laughing, Emma waiting, sitting in the light and the sun, the plush leather seat radiating warmth. He was leaning, awkwardly leaning over the consol between them *(finally)* sweeping her into a lemony-vanilla kiss so skilled that she almost protested.

"You're an old hand at this, aren't you?"

"What do you mean?" he said, simultaneously unbuttoning her blouse with one hand and pushing aside her skirt with the other.

She couldn't speak the word. Instead, she said, "The clandestine."

"I'd like to fuck you on the stage of the Citadel. That's how public I'd like to be. We could put on such a show. We'd set the theatre on fire."

"Kind of kinky." Her voice was questioning rather than judgemental.

He pulled back, sat up, stared out the windshield. "Do you want to go back now?"

"That wasn't - no. I . . . ."

"If you're not comfortable. . . ."

She was anything but comfortable. "I want to be with you." She said, "But you have to realize I'm new at this kind of thing."

"This kind of thing?" he laughed. Though she did not have to reach out to touch him, he felt as far from her as when she stood watch outside his house.

"Maybe we should go back."

"You liked it in the restaurant, all those people around."

"I don't know that I did." He looked amused, superior. His hand was on her hair; a finger traced the outline of her lips. "Robert. . . ."

"Sshh. Listen, all you have to do is relax, give in, shut off that critical part of your brain." His hand dropped, slipped under her blouse and bra. He spoke into her ear: promises, suggestions, what he could do to her, she to him, together, with others, exciting her with word as well as touch. He pressed a button, and she was dropping, falling back with the seat, laid out.

Hold me, touch me, love me/now

He hiked himself awkwardly to her side, his tongue caressing, speaking, so the words, the idea of the forbidden penetrated her mind. And injected panic. Who was he who spoke such things? And what was she doing at his mercy? Juris, steadfast Juris. It wasn't as if she was deprived, unsatisfied. No, they'd been adventuresome, experimental, especially the first years. What kind of man gave voice to these dark desires? Her dark desires. Who saw into the shadows of her mind, who caught her most ephemeral fantasies, transitory images in the flux of consciousness and said let us make these impulses flesh. Who – her heart beat faster with excitement and fear. The smell of warm leather, of skin in the sun. Say you'd, his ragged breath in her ear, for me. Flesh white in the brightness. And she gave herself to the current, to the river of colours: blues, greens, mauves, silver in her veins flesh energy light

flux
eternal change

a reflecting pool of floating water flowers

Emma was still Aida, still an adolescent when she first (at the Museum of Modern Art) saw three of Monet's enormous canvases in his water lily series. On entering the room where they were hung, she was overcome, swept away. When her mother suggested that they move on to the cafe, "I'm dying for a smoke," Aida answered with a half-strangled moan.

"Aida, come on. My feet are killing me."

"I could stay here forever," Aida finally managed to say. "I could look and look."

Ten years later when she came to choose a thesis topic, it seemed natural that the subject be Monet. The critical attitude towards his work was in the process of changing; what had been dismissed as too boneless and casual for a place in the canon was being re-evaluated as the backbone of the present, the precursor of Abstract Expressionism, the master of colour-field. And Emma Avendemis would be part of the rehabilitation of his reputation. Since the water garden paintings had already been the focus of much recent study, she chose Monet's twenty canvas sequence on Rouen Cathedral, his attempt in his words to do "architecture without using lines or contours." The sequence recorded the effects of light, atmosphere, and weather on the cathedral: the reality of nature as experienced against the non-natural and man-made.

And, though Emma already missed the print shop, the following months were among the happiest she could remember. She spent them at her carrel in the library, her tiny residence apartment or travelling (often with Juris) to New York, Washington, Boston, and Williamstown to see those canvases most closely at hand. She spent them, lost in work, lost in Monet's paint strokes, his vibrating colours, his limitlessness. And she discovered that, despite what had been claimed, Monet was not just an eye, the sequence was not just about the going and coming of light, but the experience of consciousness (sight and feeling and thought) through and within time.

The American painter Whistler accused Monet of "never delimiting his forms, where nature often delimits."

Monet answered, "Yes, doubtless nature does, but light never does."

Roth seemed pleased with the first three chapters of Emma's thesis. He began to speak of her future. What would be best? A fellowship? An apprenticeship to a major museum? MOMA might have an opening in the next few months. He could give Maddle a call. Or did she want to stay in Chicago? She had a boyfriend, didn't she? The Art Institute had nothing this year, but if she was willing to wait. . . .

"I'm not sure," Emma said.

"Of course. Finish the thesis. There's no rush. You can decide where later." Roth was sprawled out on his chair, his long legs stretching to the centre of his office.

Emma stared at his cowboy booted feet. "I love it. This work. But I would like to try and go back to making prints. That's what I've always wanted to do. I told you, didn't I?" She looked into his face. "I promised my parents that . . . but. . . ."

"You think you can do it?"

"Well – I don't know – I mean, I hope so. I. . . ."

"Make it new? More, part of the tradition of the new?"

"You saw my undergraduate work?"

"Indeed. Undergraduate."

"Nothing else?"

"Pretty, some of it. The ones with the ethnicy patterns were the worst."

"I did those in my first, no, my second year. I was eighteen."

"I'm not trying to discourage you, but you must be realistic. It's not easy. You either make art that's part of the living tradition, or you make kitsch. And in that case, it would be better to do something else, something useful and necessary."

Discouragement, a gray and gritty fog, dropped over Emma. She could barely see her professor, and his words sounded muffled. "I don't believe in all that historic determinism," she said more to herself than him. "Art manifesting itself through the march of great men. At least not just that."

It was the first time she had challenged him, challenged the sprawling, massive presence that he was in her mind. But once started she could not seem to stop. She began to question each one of his pronouncements. She believed – of course, she believed – form, texture, flatness, and self referentiality; yet, she had doubts: unimportant, niggling doubts that she pounced on and inflated. And what proved more harmful, where she once kept silent, she now answered back.

"Will I see you at the demonstration?" Roth asked casually.

"Me? You haven't noticed yet? I stay away from that stuff. I'm not interested. I don't care. They've even dropped the draft, for goodness sake. What do you want?"

"I should ask you that. You do surprise me."

"Good. Why should everyone think alike."

He was looking at her in a different way – inspecting. "You think it has nothing to do with you, but it does. You know what they say. Either you're part of the problem or part of the solution."

"I wish," Emma said.

"He's as naive as the others," she told Juris.

"Americans," Juris said with a slight shrug of his shoulders. He and Emma laughed partly at themselves.

"Commie dupes," she said, and they laughed again.

And despite repeated material destruction, deadly plagues and frequent humiliating defeats by a succession of foreign invaders, the Latvians have managed to survive with their cultural identity intact.

Sellers, *Latvia*

Emma did not hesitate when Juris asked her to marry him. She knew it was the right thing. Though he was only a few years older than she, and he was neither rich nor *(thank goodness)* given to sermons, he was her Mr. Knightly with all the important qualities: honesty, integrity, discernment, gentleness, and background. He did not know her from childhood. He hadn't watched her grow up, but he knew her so well that it felt as if he had.

His parents and hers were pleased by their engagement.

Good family, said Maya Zeps.

It's appropriate, said Andrejs Zeps.

My older brother, rest his soul, courted her, said Laila Avendemis talking of Maya. She was a beauty then, imagine.

The father's stiff-necked, said Harijs Avendemis, and the mother's a bit batty. You'll do fine.

I suspect they don't have a plethora of friends, added Harijs, which should help keep the guest list reasonable.

Oh Daddy, said Emma, how can you use the word reasonable in connection with your plans. She was enough of a child of the sixties to be embarrassed by the thought of a full-blown formal wedding. She and Juris had spoken of something simple and stylish; after all the ceremony wasn't that important, they were already married in their hearts. But her mother had cried and his had agreed: there must be a proper celebration. And the planning slipped, like that, from Emma's hand.

Listen, what does my little girl want?

Flowers. I was thinking of lots of flowers, Emma said casually.

And her father turned her suggestion into an extravagance, filling their house with every bloom in the neighbourhood, taxing the florist for the church and the reception (at the best and oldest hotel in town). She was touched by the gesture. And, as the three days of festivities started, she declared herself resigned. "It's kind of nice," she told Velga, her matron of honour.

"Kind of inevitable, " Velga said. "Tribal rites." Velga had got married the year before and was already separated. She was playing the voice of doom. "You'll be sorry," she'd mutter in Emma's ear. "Men are pigs. You can't trust any of them."

The two hundred and fifty guests came from all over the world: her godmother, whom she'd never seen before, came from Australia, cousins from South Africa and Germany, family friends from Texas and Washington and Montreal. Emma did not follow the general rule that the bride must not look like herself but a figure of make believe: a southern belle or a fairy tale princess. No tiara, no veil, only a Victorian lace dress she could almost wear again. "You look innocent," Velga said, "the basic requirement. A book full of blank pages."

Emma and Juris did follow Latvian traditions, Emma with a sprig of myrtle pinned to her department store dress, Juris with the sash of his Latvian fraternity, blue, white, and yellow over his rented tuxedo. His fraternity was ancient and Germanic, dedicated to the venerable traditions of fencing and drinking, drinking and fencing. At the conclusion of the wedding, the four fraternity brothers who'd acted as ushers interrupted Emma and Juris's recession in order to present Emma ceremoniously with a large bouquet of red roses, bound with a blue, white, and yellow ribbon.

Later on, the same four followed a less charming tradition. They kidnapped Emma from the reception, surrounding her when she came out of the restroom with Velga. "No guys, let's not do this," Emma said, as one of them gestured to the exit. "I won't go. Medieval idiocy."

"One way or the other," Rolfs said, tackling her at the knees and flinging her over his shoulder.

Emma shrieked. "Call Juris. Velga, quick."

But Velga did not move. She was smiling, smug. "You would get married." She held the door open for Rolfs and his gang. "See you later," she waved goodbye to Emma.

"Bitch," Emma yelled. Then, to Rolfs. "Put me down. You're wrinkling my dress. . . . Rolfs, I'll walk. I will."

So Emma spent half of her wedding reception locked in a seedy motel room. Two of the guys stood guard outside; Rolfs and Bill sat on the bed. They offered her vodka, rum, soda pop. "Don't be dumb," she said. She tried to watch *To Have and Have Not* on TV. Rolfs and Bill drank and smoked and laughed, boasted of other exploits and adventures. They didn't expect a ransom, they told Emma, it wasn't the old days. It was just a little joke. That was all.

"Shush," Emma said repeatedly, "what a pain you two are." But she was laughing, laughing at Bill, hair combed over one eye, doing Bacall and Harry trying to be Bogart when Juris shoved aside the guards and began banging on the door. She aimed a blow at Rolfs' chest, knocking him off the bed. "My hero has arrived," she said.

In 1940, 78 percent of the population of Latvia was Latvian, in 1979, 53.7 percent.

Two months after the wedding, Andrejs Zeps sent Emma and Juris each a letter. *Dearest Aida* was how he began the one for Emma. *You*
have understood how pleased I was and am that my son chose you for his wife. You have the qualities necessary for a long and lasting marriage.
I am an old man and an experienced one, and I write to offer you the fruits of that experience. He scattered his advice through four pages.
Don't be rigid, be patient, for patience is the key that
turns every lock.
A marriage is nothing without children.
And they must be brought up to know and respect
their homeland.
The mother transmits the values.
Let the nursery rhymes, let the lullabies be Latvian.
Keep the flame of the hearth and the flame of our
culture burning.

When Harry was still a toddler and Andy barely launched into childhood, Juris and Emma took them on a leisurely trip through France and Germany. They spent four days in Rouen: eating apple pancakes, drinking calvados, walking up and down the hills, and (they calculated later) conceiving Michael. They visited the gardens at Giverny, the site of Flaubert's home at Croisset, and, of course, the cathedral, which was not what she'd expected, blackened as it was from pollution and damaged from the war, many of the stained glass windows replaced with clear glass. Still, it bore many layers of human meaning: witness to an age of belief and subject of numberless paintings and lithographs even before Monet began to paint. Close by was the spot where Joan of Arc burned. Across the square stood Au Printemps, a superior department store where Emma shopped each afternoon while the boys took their naps. They left the city with numerous treasures: for Emma, a red umbrella with a carved wood handle, a silk shawl with a flower pattern, a cashmere cardigan, a blue wool skirt, and green walking shoes; for the boys, soft cotton underwear and snug fitting jeans, and for Juris, grey, thickwale corduroy slacks.

INTERRUPTION

Rouen, home to Pascal and Corneille and Flaubert, relates to my city, my Edmonton, the same way that one of Monet's paintings, priming, *ebauche* (or lay-in) and elaboration, layer over layer, relates to the Dorothy Knowles watercolour that hangs in my living room, the same way that Flaubert's *Madame Bovary* relates to this text.

These days we are suspicious of claims of universality and genius, suspicious of the sacred monsters, the dead white men we were once taught to venerate. To find a small space, a blank page on which the words will form. To find a quiet spot, away from the old cultural clatter, where our voices can be heard – where I can hear my own voice – we must dare *(Flaubert)*. We must thrust aside *(c'est moi.)*. We must shout down. *(Scram, Gustave.)*

We must.
Yet
Yet to the 10th.*(Get real.)*

To push Flaubert aside is to deprive myself – of his work and of what his work has meant to others. How many books have been written on *Madame Bovary*? Hundreds? Thousands? And not just works of criticism or scholarship. Just in the last few years, an English writer has spun a crypto-novel, a Peruvian presidential candidate a confession, both from Flaubert's texts. Nothing I have read, says the South American, has meant so much to me. And his reading, the meaning he extracted from *Madame*

Bovary, and Barnes's reading and James's reading and the critics' reading and each of the other individual, often different, readings add layers of value and authority to the book.

The few times that Juris allowed himself to think about what there was between his wife and that man, he felt as if a mist, white and thick, had crept up and surrounded him. He felt disoriented, directionless, unable to see in front or beside him. He was caught, yet what held him? Nothing that he could touch: a faint sensation of dampness, of air. So he stood still and waited for clarity.

He viewed Emma's illness (for so he diagnosed it) as partly genetic. Latvians, his father used to say almost proudly, are never satisfied, suggesting by his tone that they understood more than the cheerful Americans. The precipitating factor was viral. Common enough, he told himself, and not mortal. Such illnesses are self-limiting. Patience.

He found himself thinking of his mother and father. Together yet separate through the years, two walls: her obsession and his between them. *Remember your wife is not your servant but your equal,* his father had written. *Be steadfast. Be patient. You will be tried. Such is the nature of life.* Juris found the paternal letter of marital advice at the bottom of his documents box (along with the deed to what was once the Zeps country home in Kurzeme, near the sea). For his father, marriage was eternal: a vow given before God, given to God. *I know what you are thinking, son. I can hear your voice. 'Who are you to give advice?' But listen, whether your Mother and I have been happy is irrelevant. Whatever we are here for it is not happiness (which comes at random or not at all). Your mother and I still love, still hold fast. I remember an old poem:*

The ring so worn as you behold
So thin, so pale, is yet of gold:
The passion such it was to prove;
Worn with life's cares
Love was yet love

Family, work, community, culture, it all comes back to you and her. What else is there?

Emma gloried, she revelled in her role as mistress. Over and over, in tones of wonder, she told herself "I have a lover." Driving Harry to hockey practice. "I have a lover." Washing the kitchen floor. "I have a lover." Staring into the meat counter of the IGA, trying to decide if she could face hamburgers again. "I have a lover." The phrase was her talisman, her illicit charm; she imagined it glittering at the base of her throat, gold curliqued letters, dangling from a chain at her wrist. She might look like the most average of housewives: dull, predictable, jeans and ski jacket. But underneath, underneath, she wore a secret uniform – cobwebs of lace, whispers of silk. She was not what she seemed. "I have more than one mask."

"You've changed sides," Frances said one afternoon at the skating rink. "You used to believe children needed their mother."

"My kids are fine. They're fantastic."

"Of course," Frances said with one of her tight smiles. "If you are pleased with the care they're getting. I have heard that you've used Melissa Bailey. Did I ever tell you about the experience the Smiths had with her?"

"I think I've heard it several times. She's just a backup, anyway. Look, I gotta go. I was just picking Michael up. Mike, right now."

"We haven't seen you for months. How about coming for tea tomorrow?"

"Sorry. Not this week. Too hectic. Michael, last chance." And Emma hurried away, pulling her son by the hand, anxious to escape any more comments on her Byzantine childcare arrangements, which included two playschools and three different student sitters. And still tended to fall through, as they had the day before, trapping her in the house, denying her a planned drive with Robert to the lake. Emma had to wait a week until his schedule and hers (or rather her sitter's) coincided.

"I can take some time between two and three thirty Wednesday."

"The boys get out at 3:20, and I'm not covered sitter-wise Wednesdays."

Could we try? Could you fit in? How about? Snatched time, stolen time, secret time. "I have more than one mask."

Suddenly, inevitably, she would be repulsed by the pettiness, the sordidness, the duplicity. Fake, she would mutter at her reflection in the mirror. *Liar, liar, pants on fire.* Wasn't that the truth. Probably where the phrase came from. *Pants on fire* leads to *liar, liar.*

Emma bought Juris an armload of flowers for his nameday, irises and gladioli and roses. She baked a *klingeris* cake and served it with a bottle of Perrier-Jouet. "Remember that restaurant in Rouen," she said. "Two bottles. What a hangover."

She was leaning over, pouring more champagne, one hand on the table for balance. He covered the hand with his. Their fingers intertwined; his thumb turned her gold band. "Thank you, Aida," he said in Latvian.

After that first time in the Mercedes, Emma couldn't bear for Lamartine to undress her. She'd break away (I'll do it), turning it into a show, so he wouldn't suspect. Letting her clothes slither to the floor. Posing just a little. There was nothing natural or comfortable about their couplings. Each time he touched her, for the first few seconds, she had to stifle the urge to push his hands away, to scream.

She would bite her lip, steel herself until the sensations, the excitement, started. Until she was carried off on a flood made more intense, more frenzied, by a prickling sediment of pain.

Love me/Fill me/With ecstasy/Now

Her body was still humming happily from a quickie in Lamartine's office (in the swivel chair, on the desk), when she ran into Janie. She was on the down and Janie on the up escalator in ManuLife Place, and Janie yelled, "Emma, wait, coming down." Over cappuccino in a nearby cafe, Janie stared at Emma, "Have to admit this working has done you good. You look terrific."

"I enjoy it." Emma tried not to look too smug.

"A challenge?"

"Not that. No, it's a change. A break. Eventually, I'll find something else."

"I'm just glad you got over that man."

"What man?"

"Lamartine. Remember, in the summer?"

"Oh, that. That was nothing. A puff of air."

"I'm glad. He's horrible and he's rude." Janie's blue eyes seemed charged with meaning.

"I wouldn't know."

"He got you your job. . . . I was worried 'cause . . . he uses people." Why did Janie feel impelled to deliver these tiresome warnings? What was it about Robert that had set her off? Unless. . . . Emma's stomach lurched. Wholesome, wheat germ Janie? She needed to be reassured immediately. She couldn't just sit and make nice. She threw out an excuse and started to rush back to his office. Janie? Impossible. Janie? In the elevator, she pressed the button for his floor but, when it began to rise, she pressed lobby. She couldn't call him out of his meeting. She would have to phone later. If she could catch him before he rushed off to the Calgary airbus. He'd warned her against leaving too many messages with his secretary. But this was important – an emergency. And if she didn't, it could be a couple of days. And she couldn't wait, not with this feeling in her stomach. She had to hear him say he had never given Janie a second glance.

"I am his mistress," she said to herself. "He is my lover." But she was not soothed, for she felt no more in control, and – in a way – no closer, than she had when she stood outside his house night after night. Mistress of what? She mocked herself. In command of what? A fantasy with his face. Who knows how many others he had stashed away? Not Janie, please, not her.

What could she be sure of? He liked to talk to her. She knew that. He called at odd moments, from his car phone or in between appointments. (Juris was usually at the lab, and the rare times he answered Robert pretended it was work related.) He would tell her about his latest victory, in squash or business. "I made mincemeat out of him," he'd say. "The chump didn't know what hit him." "I finessed the deal. You should have seen me."

He told her – in detail – about all the incompetence, stupidity, and venality he had to deal with that day. "Don't get me started on this council." He discussed his future plans: "I would like my own hockey team." He confessed mistakes; "I'll never trust like *that* again." And he did ask her advice about movies and records and clothes. "You keep up with things." "You've got taste." He even asked her to choose two paintings for his office. Doing that had given her a high that lasted a complete week.

(Andy had commented on her good spirits and sudden flurry of baking. "I know it's fun, Mom, but we like bought cookies better.")

204

What else was Emma sure of? For now, Robert wanted her body and her company. "I've been horny all day thinking of you." As she licked his nipples slowly, teasingly, "God, you're a sexy little bitch." He seemed surprised, excited by her compliance. Once, when he was talking to his wife on the phone, he wrote Emma a note: *show yourself to me*, and she had obeyed, improvised. "You're too much – amazing." She wanted to be more than too much; she wanted him to demand more, push more, farther ever farther. One afternoon, when she came and came and came, he said, "I bet we could set a world record. Does Guinness carry this category?"

Emma ignored Lamartine's warning and left a message with Lamartine's secretary. He didn't call back. That night after Juris had gone to bed, she phoned the Palliser, the Westin, finding him finally at the Delta Bow Valley.

"I was asleep," he said sounding irritated and wide awake.

"You didn't call." She was whispering.

"I was in a rush. You knew that."

"I had to talk to you." She spoke quickly, before she lost her courage. "I had to know about you and Jane Fischer."

There was a long silence. "Who?" he said.

"I know you know her. She worked on the telethon last year. I know. . . ."

"So . . . I know who you mean."

"Did you and her. . . ."

"You're being ridiculous." His voice was cold, nasty. "I don't go for the mousy housewife type."

"Thanks."

She felt angry, not reassured, angry, confused, and lost, not knowing how to read his words or actions. Who was he?

The next time they were together, when they were done

and he started to get up, she grabbed his arm and held on. "Not yet."

"I have to go." But he let himself fall back into the motel pillows.

"Always such a rush," she said, running a finger slowly over his chin.

"I am kind of tired." He stared up at the ceiling. She focused on his profile until she could see the floating contact lens.

"Why don't you pop your lenses out and have a rest."

"Can't. Meeting."

"You know, I've checked out every square inch of you, but you've never taken your lenses out. I've never seen your naked eyeball. Do you realize how weird that is?"

"Not today," he said. Emma rolled off the bed and grabbed his shirt. Holt Renfrew Classic label. Thin blue and white stripes. His smell – lemon and vanilla with the sightest undertow of sweat. The material was smooth, luxurious Eygptian cotton. It felt good on her back. "I've had my R & R for today," he said. She fastened the sleeves with his heavy gold cuff links. "You were the one who had to rush off the other week." She pulled his French bikini briefs, then the Italian wool trousers up over her hips. They were only a little too long. She tightened his leather belt to the last notch, bunching the wool around her waist. Thrusting her hands into his empty pockets, she strode around the room, imitating his confident step. She tried to imagine a weight, an extra presence, between her legs. What would it be like? She watched herself in the mirror, reproducing his habit of lifting his left shoulder ever so slightly in a near-invisible tic, his way of sticking out his lower lip before a grimace.

"Gotta deal, gotta go," she whispered at her reflection, hearing his voice. He was watching her, his eyes wary.

When she picked up his Hugo Boss tie and suit jacket, he asked, "What are you doing?"

"You should take me out. For lunch. For a walk."

"Why? You don't enjoy this?"

"We could talk. Get to know each other."

"Oh we know – more than enough. Of course, we'll have lunch. But we have to be cautious. For both our sakes."

"I'll chance it," she said. Though when she imagined a scenario with her and Robert out, his arm around her, and their running into Juris *(It can't be)*, the idea sent her into a panic.

Lamartine's obvious desire wasn't enough to keep her from the swamps of anxiety. She would lie in her bed at night sinking, sinking into the ooze. And in desperation, she would reach out for Juris, silent Juris; she would cling to him until he turned to her. They hung on to each other; without a word, they hung on.

Robert did not say the words of love that she was waiting to hear, that she needed to hear to justify what they were doing. He would not fantasize a future for them. And though she knew they would never have that future, Emma wanted to be lulled by the idea; she wanted to play let's pretend – you and I.

She wanted him to offer her a tropical isle and sweet rum drinks and the two of them walking along the beach, hand in hand, like in the commercials. She wanted him to promise an antique-filled hotel and Paris and bouquets of spring violets and *La Tour D'Argent* with the Eiffel Tower as decoration and a Chanel suit and love and the Orient Express and Venice and the Grand Canal and a gondola ride and the moon. *Fly me to,* she thought.

Though even while she thought it, even while she

daydreamed, an inner voice said, would you really want to travel with him? Wouldn't his deals and businesses grow tiresome? His conversation – eventually – boring?

I'll teach him, she answered the calm, nasty voice, broaden his horizons, introduce him to culture beyond Andrew Lloyd Webber and Neil Simon. And she lost herself in new daydreams: the two of them in the Louvre, at La Scala and the Barzibon.

Lamartine didn't seem aware of what a good companion, what an appropriate wife she could be. Why couldn't he see? She'd been educated to partner a sucessful man. Not like his bleached blonde wife with her community college degree. Figure it out, dodo, she thought.

"Aren't I special to you? You never say," she complained, craving words of appreciation, of praise.

"Sure I do." He sounded amused. "You have the wickedest mouth ever." His hand on the back of her neck, guiding her down.

Another time. "You never buy me anything."

"What do you mean? For services rendered?"

"Pig."

"And don't you love it."

"A little token of your esteem."

"A payoff."

"Why don't you take me somewhere? We can think up excuses. A miniature grand tour."

She brought up the idea of a trip each time they saw each other. "Come on, take me to New York." He began to look evasive or slightly irritated. If he had questioned her, she would have had to admit that it would not be easy for her either to leave the boys or to find a cover story. Instead, he muttered that he was busy, maybe next month or the month after.

"Wouldn't you like to spend some real time with me?

All those things you promised."

"What things?" He was hurriedly dressing.

"We'd need time, a lot more time."

"Never enough for you, eh?" He was staring into the mirror, knotting his tie.

"We have to stop rushing."

"I don't know. Urgency. Keeps us hot. No, it is too bad we have to be so careful. If I wasn't so recognizable. . . . I've always wanted to try a quickie in an elevator. Or you could go down on me as I drove along a country road."

"You see! And you're thinking small. There's so much more. Don't you remember all you suggested? We . . . we could explore all our fantasies. Right to the very bottom. Just imagine – New York."

Emma did go to New York, but not with Lamartine. A phone call at five one morning and she was packing. Her mother had suffered a stroke. Her father was in Latvia on his first trip back, and the neighbour had been unable to contact him. A phone call and she was away, dropping years and roles as she flew across the continent. Before midnight, she walked into her mother's room.

"Mother," her voice was a croak. "It's me – Aida."

Her mother lay immobile, her face the colour of the dingy sheets. "Let her sleep," the nurse said. "She's stabilized. Get some rest."

So she went to her old home, silent and dark, and walked through the tidy rooms, expecting – at any moment – a voice, a whiff of cigarette smoke, the smell of bacon and coffee. She lay down on her old bed in her old room, which was still so much the same (new wallpaper, they never liked the mauve and peach paint she'd wanted): same furniture, carpet, shelf of stuffed animals, a teddy bear holding a burgundy and white flag, same framed museum posters, and two of her early prints. Not bad, she thought, way back when. She did not sleep; she would doze for a few minutes only to be jerked awake to her pounding heart, to shadows upon shadows, to dark shapes simultaneously familiar and strange. Her muscles were tight, her mind twitched.

The next day, her head ached with exhaustion. She spoke to Dr. Macdonald, who had taken out her tonsils and prescribed her first birth control pills. "The damage is extensive," he said. "Be prepared."

The specialist offered more hope. "A woman's brain is more flexible," he said. "If this had been your father, I would be more pessimistic."

Emma sat in an armchair, next to her mother's bed. She sat with her head resting against the back of the chair, watching the bright green numbers on the machines, the everchanging numbers that recorded her mother's heartbeat, two kinds of blood pressure, and respiration rate. Life measured: life reduced into a sequence of everchanging numbers. Sometimes, she made herself look at her mother or touch her hand. "Fight. You can," she would say. The nurse was constantly in and out: intensive care, though the service, the observation was to the machines rather than the woman. He would try to chat, aiming casual questions at Emma. She would answer in a word. She could not make polite conversation. She would not.

She was keeping watch, immobilized by her mother's immobility. Numb. Stiff face, twisted mouth. Green on black – numbers. Grey-rooted brown hair. Numbers. Green on black. Laila's eyes opened. "Mother, can you hear me. It's me. Mother?" And one eye winked.

Hours passed. The nurses changed shift. The

numbness was cracking, split by anger. Emma called Juris and the boys. "She's coming round. She looks at me." Beneath her preoccupation, she was thinking of Lamartine, replaying certain moments in her mind, over and over. Two days before her trip, she'd discovered that he had left for Palm Springs. He hadn't told her he was going; he hadn't even warned her that he was considering it. She knew what that meant.

Two weeks earlier, he had given her a gold chain necklace. Foolishly, she'd been touched, accepting it as a late Christmas gift. (She'd told Juris that it was costume, and she'd bought it herself.) Now she saw its true significance. And her anger added to her paralysis.

That night, Emma drank half a bottle of her father's Scotch. The next day she sat and sat, contemplating her mother and her anger. She had to admit to herself that she was no longer under Lamartine's spell. Besides, part of her had always had doubts, had always been critical. But this did not make his defection any easier to take. She had given herself to him, debased herself, betrayed Juris. And for what? She'd been nothing to him: a diversion, a toy. She must show him that she was not so easily dismissable. She would phone his wife. She would make a scene in his office. She would make him – somehow – make him – what? Give her her due. At least, that.

The machines pulsed green and black. Her mother stared at her. The nurse shouted, "Laila, we are going to move you into a more comfortable room. Your condition is improving." Emma's mother moved her left hand very slowly over to her right. She made a sign as if she were trying to lift her right hand. Her face was fierce with sadness and disgust.

"I know. It's hard. Really hard. But, Mother, you can fight back. You can and will. You'll move again. You have to."

They were in the new, less technological room – Emma had just returned from supper, yogurt and coffee in the cafeteria – when her father appeared at the door. He looked frightened, rumpled and grey and old and frightened.

Emma's first impulse was to speak in their usual bantering tone. But she suppressed her "welcome back, Pops." She crossed the room to enfold him in a hug. "Thank goodness," she said.

The next few days blurred one into another. Emma and her father took turns staying with Laila, watching the therapists move her about in range-of-motion exercises, watching the doctors and nurses sauntering in and out, consulting, prognosticating. They took turns brushing her hair and rubbing cream into her dry, sore skin. And whenever her eyes were open, they talked and questioned and cajoled.

Emma returned from a walk in the park to hear her father say, "You should see what they've done to our house. You would cry, Laila. Our beautiful house – a ruin. Torn apart for firewood. Torn apart. Everything gone."

"Father, can I speak to you over here, please?"

"What's wrong? There hasn't been some bad news? Did they lie. . . ?"

"No, Dad. What you were saying; it isn't what she needs to hear."

"No, no. It is exactly what she needs to hear." He raised his voice. "Exactly."

"Tell her the hopeful part. How attitudes are changing, how the courage to resist is growing."

"So she will worry about the inevitable slaughter? Your mother and I have seen too much. . . . We can no longer deal in hope."

Emma shook her head. She could not find the right

words. Or any words. Her father sat down again and took his wife's clawed right hand. "It comes to this," he said with his ironic smile.

Finally, Emma said, "No. Things are changing. I've seen on TV. . . . There's a chance. For Latvia, another chance."

"Listen to her," he said to Laila. "Your daughter who wouldn't teach her children Latvian. Gloat a little. You're entitled."

Emma talked to her mother about the daily details of family life: lost socks and new blinds and how Michael wouldn't eat anything but cheese and mayonnaise sandwiches for lunch *everyday,* and how Andrejs answered them in Latvian for a good three weeks after camp last summer. "Juris hasn't gone back to speaking English with them. He's trying to hold to the Latvian with all three. . . . With me sometimes too. It's been a surprise," she said.

She talked about her childhood, about Brooklyn and their friends. I remember, she would begin, I remember. Do you? Do you . . . remember?

Then, as if conjured up by the memories, Velga was there, walking towards Emma's table in the cafeteria. "Is it really you?" Emma asked, for as her friend drew closer, she looked less like Velga. The pose was the same: jaunty, but the lines of the face were blurred, smudged by wrinkles and incipient jowls. Her tawny hair (dirty blonde they used to call it) was bleached platinum, her face deeply tanned. Even her eyes were different: wary, shrewd. We've both got middle-aged, Emma thought, as she stood to hug her, but I do look younger than you.

"Who else? Of course, it's me." Velga tugged at her short skirt and sat down. "I heard about your Mum. From mine. A real bummer."

"Umm. It's been horrible." Emma said. "But she is improving. And it's great to see you, Velga. It's been a few years. How long do you think?"

"Look, I'm called Diane now. O.K? Gives me the creeps – Velga. You were preggers, Sweetie. Last time."

"And you were Kate." As she spoke Emma remembered the argument they had had that last time, sparked off when Velga made fun of Emma's domesticity. "Aren't you a little bored?" she'd asked.

"That was Shane, my boyfriend then. He liked the name, thought it suited me. When he went. . . ." Velga/Diane shrugged. "I'm gonna get myself a coffee. Wanna refill?"

So over coffee that managed to taste both watery and metallic, Emma and Velga caught up, each providing the other with a speedy tour of the terrain covered in the most recent stages of their life journeys. Velga/Diane had gone through several lovers and one husband. "Usual jerks and fuck ups." She'd done some acting, a play off broadway, a small part in a film. Kate was a good name for an actress. But then the parts dried up. "They said I couldn't play ingenue anymore. They wouldn't let me try. The pits. Finally I went back to singing. Now I'm with this band. Good guys. We're playing lounges, clubs. This producer said he'd come and see us in Albany. And you never know. . . ."

And money? She had some luck there. She drove packages from Miami to New York or Philadelphia to Washington, say once a month, and they – these guys – paid her very well.

"Oh Velga, it sounds –"

"Oh Aida, don't you know? A girl's got to do what a girl's got to do?" Velga gave her one of her old taunting looks.

214

Yet when Emma took her turn (she had wanted for so long to tell someone, anyone, about her and Lamartine) Velga/Diane expressed no amazement, no "I was wrong about you." "The usual story," she said.

"Not usual for me."

"Juris is a good guy," Velga said.

"Him and his test tubes. Quite a couple. No, you're right. I know. Anyway, I quit my job before I left," she said. "The pay was peanuts." Afterwards, Emma regretted confiding in Velga. For where she had once vicariously enjoyed her friend's adventures, she no longer had any interest in the continual flutter from man to job to man. She felt nothing for the woman, the "Diane" Velga had become. Their friendship had ended a long time before. And Emma felt foolish for trying to revive it artificially by offering up her secrets.

A little more than a year later, Emma was flying back to visit her mother for the third time. Laila was much better. She could walk with a cane. She could speak, though often she could not find the word she wanted. She would stutter out a sound, shake her head, repeat the sound – again and again until finally she'd manage to nudge herself on. Emma felt grateful that, despite the changes, Laila was still with them, still Laila, cynical and proud. But sitting on that plane, Emma was also irritated. The flight had been stuck on the runway for two hours in Minneapolis. She was going to arrive in the middle of the night. She was drinking Scotch and flipping through magazines when she found one with Sandra Dee on the cover. Her face was no longer a pretty confection. The woman looked strained, almost puffy. Inside, the former star told her story, a common story of child abuse, alcoholism, and anorexia. Emma felt herself turning back into Aida, back into that adolescent girl who had looked at Sandra Dee on the screen and yearned to have her cute face, her compact body, her privileged American life. If I could only have a waist that small, she used to think to herself. And now she discovered that Sandra Dee herself did not have a waist that small, except through starvation, except through a perversion of normal impulses. Emma's eyes prickled with tears. She felt cheated, lied to, betrayed.

And, at that moment, tired and teary, she wanted, she needed to talk to the only person who could understand how she felt: Velga. The old Velga, not the woman with the aging face. The Velga that had sat with her on the stoop and giggled. The Velga that had played with her in the safe place under the table, while all around the adults sang and argued, carped and cried.

Emma was floating away on this gentle wave of nostalgia when, without warning, she was pulled under, engulfed, whirled by a cold, turbulent undercurrent. *Here is Kurzeme/ Here is Vidzeme /Here Latgale.* She felt the loss – for the first time she felt it in her arms and legs and heart and stomach, salt on the skin, on the tongue – the loss of the country she had never known, never seen, the loss of the very idea of that country.

Received Ideas, 1992
I hear where you're coming from.
Say what you mean.
"When I use a word," Humpty Dumpty said, in a rather scornful tone, **"it means exactly what I choose it to mean – neither more nor less."**

Flaubert gave his life to perfect his style, because he thought language was inadequate (a cracked kettle) to express our feelings or to describe the reality beyond ourselves. For him, Emma Bovary's stupidity springs from her believing that the books she reads reproduce a certain world. She does not realize that they are arbitrary and refer only to themselves. He wanted to achieve a pure style, independent of content ("without external attachments"). Just as a century later the Abstract Expressionists strove to produce painting without outside subject or content. Flaubert hated clichés and the tendency of language to become a series of commonplaces. (He ignored, as Sartre says, the common shared feeling clichés represent.) A warrior of the pen, he attacked and ridiculed mercilessly. And he worked and worked and worked to make his language, his words, beautiful and translucent.

But the more that one "works" language, the more one examines, plays, manipulates words, the more opaque they become. Each utterance, if one thinks long and deeply enough, is shown to be inadequate, even banal. (Emma Bovary, c'est nous, indeed.) In the end, one is left with the materiality of words. What could be more appropriate for our material age, our material world, our material girl? Step up to the zeitgeist.

Remember that modern art gallery I mentioned at the beginning? The last time I visited, words were everywhere – illegible phrases written on canvas, contextless sentences scrawled in pencil under photographs and, in clear printing, "Shit. Art is dead" over a yellow grid. The main exhibit was an installation piece by a German artist which involved a dental chair moving on a track, several piles of slashed canvases, a stone gargoyle emiting frog sounds and a row of T-shirts stamped in bold black with words. The words were grouped in ungrammatical, illogical phrases, as if they'd been put together at random by a non-speaker of English. Or as if they'd been chosen only for how they looked. A new kind of still life, the latest in material.

Before Emma flew back to Edmonton and her family, ten days or so after her mother's stroke, she went to the opening of an art exhibit on her old college campus. The show was a retrospective of Jack Nadow's career and had been mounted in celebration of his long association with the college. He was there – at the opening – surrounded by students in black and by town matrons in sequins. He looked older but not that much older. It was as if time had stood still or, at least, run in a circle. Jack's work was again being praised, again in fashion.

Emma was standing before a painting that managed, it was so thickly layered, to be almost three dimensional when Nadow suddenly spoke in her ear. "I remember. The girl with the bicycle."

"No longer a girl and no longer with bicycle."

"It comes to us all." He made a gesture at the painting. "What do you think?"

"It's almost medieval. How did you get this complexity?" They talked, moving from canvas to canvas. Nadow was attentive, ignoring, for a few minutes, all the other women for her. Why? Was it guilt? She wondered how she could introduce the subject of her collaboration and the lack of recognition. "You've given up printmaking?" she asked.

"Those were fruitful days, weren't they? What about you? Still a whiz on the press?" He'd forgotten what had happened between them. She could tell from his tone, from the look in his eyes. He thought they'd been lovers.

She told him about her switch to criticism and her uncertainty over where she fit now. "I long to be back in the studio but. . . ." She also managed to sneak in a reference to the book on his prints and the missing attribution. "I was a little confused. . . ."

Whether it was because he felt he owed her something

or because he liked her comments, Emma never knew, but Nadow submitted her name as his choice to do a catalogue for a European tour.

There is no sad ending to this story. Flaubert, *ce n'est pas moi*. And this is the last part of the twentieth century. I will not inflict an agonizing death on her and, by extension, on you and me. Emma kept her husband and children. For awhile, she and Juris did think that they would have to declare personal bankruptcy, but her parents lent them some money, and Juris took away all her credit cards, not only cutting them up but informing the companies they were to issue her no new ones.

She muddles on. I muddle on, juggling, struggling for balance.

> If only...
> If only...

Longing like the faintest of breezes stirring the water flowers, rumpling the pond skin, longing lifts within me.

Emma is ready to begin her work. Exactness, sensitivity, care, balance, all her skills have slowly returned over the last few months. She is nervous, preparing the stone, grinding off the last image. She is not alone in the studio, and the good-natured chat of the other students distracts and irritates her. She has thought about this print she will make for a long time.

But she has not imagined the finished work, only the forms, the rhythms, the questions that this method of discovery might use. She begins to etch – the sign of *Saulite*, the Sun, spread as a grid across the entire stone. She no longer hears the others, not until she has finished this given, this base. She goes through the steps: gum, acid, water, ink (amber yellow), press. Tomorrow she will scrawl and scratch the stone, so when the paper is run though some of the Sun grid will be obscured, some obliterated. Red for that layer. And words, she will write some words. NO FOLK. Black ink, definitely.